P9-BTY-737

Dangerous

Dolls

of

Delaware

Here's what readers from around the country are saying about Johnathan Rand's *AMERICAN CHILLERS:*

"I just got #10: Missouri Madhouse and it is very creepy. I had the night freakes from it!"

-Brendan F, age 9, Michigan

"My dog chewed up TERRIBLE TRACTORS OF TEXAS, and then he puked. Is that normal?"

-Carlos V., age 11, New Jersey

"Johnathan Rand's books are my favorite. They're really creepy and scary!"

-Jeremy J., age 9, Illinois

"My whole class loves your books! I have two of them and they are really, really cool."

-Katie R., age 12, California

"I never liked to read before, but now I read all the time! The 'Chillers' series is great!"

-Lauren B., age 10, Ohio

"I love AMERICAN CHILLERS because they are scary, but not too scary, because I don't want to have nightmares."

-Adrian P., age 11, Maine

"I just finished Florida Fog Phantoms. It is a freaky book! I really liked it."

-Daniel R., Michigan

"I read all of the books in the MICHIGAN CHILLERS series, and I just started the AMERICAN CHILLERS series. I really love these books!"
-Andrew K., age 13 Montana

"I have six CHILLERS books, and I have read them all three times! I hope I get more for my birthday. My sister loves them, too."
-Jaquann D., age 10, Illinois

"I just read KREEPY KLOWNS OF KALAMAZOO and it really freaked me out a lot. It was really cool!"
-Devin W., age 8, Texas

"THE MICHIGAN MEGA-MONSTERS was great! I hope you write lots more books!"
-Megan P., age 12, Kentucky

"All of my friends love your books! Will you write a book and put my name in it?"
-Michael L., age 10, Ohio

"These books are the best in the world!"
-Garrett M., age 9, Colorado

"We read your books every night. They are really scary and some of them are funny, too."
-Michael & Kristen K., Michigan

"I read THE MICHIGAN MEGA-MONSTERS in two days, and it was cool! When are you going to write one about Wisconsin?"
-John G., age 12, Wisconsin

"Johnathan Rand is my favorite author!"
-Kelly S., age 8, Michigan

"AMERICAN CHILLERS are great. I got one
for Christmas, and I loved it. Now, my sister
is reading it. When she's done, I'm going to
read it again."
-Joel F., age 13, New York

"I like the CHILLERS books because they are
fun to read. They are scary, too."
-Hannah K., age 11, Minnesota

"I read the MEGA-MONSTERS book and I
really liked it. Mr. Rand is a great writer."
-Ryan M., age 12, Arizona

"I LOVE AMERICAN CHILLERS!"
-Zachary R., age 8, Indiana

"I read your book to my little sister and
she got freaked out. I did, too!"
-Jason J., age 12, Ohio

"These books are my favorite! I love reading them!"
-Sarah N., age 10, New Jersey

"Your books are great. Please write more so I can read them."
-Dylan H., age 7, Tennessee

Don't miss these exciting, action-packed books by Johnathan Rand!

MICHIGAN CHILLERS

#1: Mayhem on Mackinac Island
#2: Terror Stalks Traverse City
#3: Poltergeists of Petoskey
#4: Aliens Attack Alpena
#5: Gargoyles of Gaylord
#6: Strange Spirits of St. Ignace
#7: Kreepy Klowns of Kalamazoo
#8: Dinosaurs Destroy Detroit
#9: Sinister Spiders of Saginaw
#10: Mackinaw City Mummies

AMERICAN CHILLERS

#1: The Michigan Mega-Monsters
#2: Ogres of Ohio
#3: Florida Fog Phantoms
#4: New York Ninjas
#5: Terrible Tractors of Texas
#6: Invisible Iguanas of Illinois
#7: Wisconsin Werewolves
#8: Minnesota Mall Mannequins
#9: Iron Insects Invade Indiana
#10: Missouri Madhouse
#11: Poisonous Pythons Paralyze Pennsylvania
#12: Dangerous Dolls of Delaware
#13: Virtual Vampires of Vermont
#14: Creepy Condors of California
#15: Nebraska Nightcrawlers
#16: Alien Androids Assault Arizona
#17: South Carolina Sea Creatures

ADVENTURE CLUB

#1: Ghost in the Graveyard
#2: Ghost in the Grand

and more coming soon!

AudioCraft Publishing, Inc.
PO Box 281
Topinabee Island, MI 49791

#12: Dangerous Dolls of Delaware

Johnathan Rand

An AudioCraft Publishing, Inc. book

This book is a work of fiction. Names, places, characters and incidents are used fictitiously, or are products of the author's very active imagination.

Graphics layout/design consultant: Scott Beard, Straits Area Printing
Honorary graphics consultant: Chuck Beard *(we miss you, Chuck)*
Editor: Diane Gurnee

Book warehouse and storage facilities provided by Clarence and Dorienne's Storage, Car Rental & Shuttle Service, Topinabee Island, MI

Warehouse security provided by Salty, Abby, & Lily Munster.

No part of this publication may be reproduced in whole or in part, or stored in a retrieval system, or transmitted in any form or by any means, electronic, mechanic, photocopying, recording, or otherwise, without written permission from the publisher. For information regarding permission, write to: AudioCraft Publishing, Inc., PO Box 281, Topinabee Island, MI 49791

Paperback ISBN 1-893699-56-0
Hardcover ISBN 1-893699-57-9

Copyright © 2003 AudioCraft Publishing, Inc. All rights reserved. AMERICAN CHILLERS is the registered trademark of AudioCraft Publishing, Inc.

Printed in USA

Second Printing - February 2005

Dangerous
Dolls
of
Delaware

Visit the official 'American Chillers' web
site at:

www.americanchillers.com

Featuring excerpts from upcoming stories, interviews,
contests, official American Chillers wearables, and *more!*
Plus, join the FREE American Chillers fan club!

1

"Find anything?" I asked as I plunged the shovel into the dirt. My brother, Spencer, was kneeling on the ground near my feet, his hands sifting through the dark, wet ground.

"Nothing yet," he said. "But I'm sure we will. Try digging deeper, Serena."

That's me. Serena Boardman. I'm twelve, and my brother, Spencer, is eleven. He was planning on going fishing in a few hours, and I was helping him dig for worms in the woods not far from our house.

And so far, we hadn't had much luck . . . but that was about to change.

Only, it wasn't worms that we would be finding.

Not today.

I'd already dug a good-sized hole. Now, I stood over it and plunged the shovel blade into the ground again, digging the hole deeper.

There was a dull thud, and the shovel stopped abruptly.

"Uh oh," I said. "We're not going any deeper here. I think I hit a root."

I pulled the shovel out of the hole. Spencer reached down, grabbed a handful of dirt, and pulled it out.

Then he stopped.

"Hey," he said, peering down into the hole. "That doesn't look like a root. Check it out."

I dropped the shovel and knelt down. Spencer and I dug with our hands, heaping the dirt beside us.

"You're right!" I exclaimed. "This isn't a root at all!"

And it wasn't. Whatever was in the ground was made of wood, but it was too smooth and flat to be a root.

Birds chirruped from the trees. The air was cool and damp, and the gray sky hinted of a coming rainstorm.

"Keep digging around the sides," Spencer said. "I think it's some kind of box."

"Like a treasure chest!" I said.

"Yeah!" Spencer exclaimed. "Maybe it's a chest full of buried treasure!"

That would be cool!

"What's a box doing way out here in the woods, buried in the ground?" I asked, pulling out another clump of dark dirt. My hands were caked with the black, clammy soil.

"You got me," Spencer replied. He reached down, grabbed a corner of the box, and pulled. The box shifted a tiny bit.

I reached down and grabbed the other side of the box.

"On three," I said. "One, two, three!"

We lifted, and the wooden box came up. It wasn't really heavy, but it sure looked old. There was no doubt that it had been in the ground for a long, long time.

"It feels empty," Spencer said as we placed the box on the ground.

"So much for buried treasure," I said.

There weren't any handles on the box, and the lid was nailed shut.

"I think I can get the blade of the shovel between the lid and the box," Spencer said, reaching for the shovel. "Then we can pry it off."

He wedged the metal blade into the thin crack and pumped the shovel up and down. The nails gave way easily, and the lid lifted.

And inside the box—

Two dolls.

Two ordinary dolls: one boy, one girl. They were old, and their clothing was faded. The girl doll's hair was falling out just above her forehead. The boy doll didn't have any hair at all. . . . just plastic that was colored brown to *look* like wavy hair.

As you can imagine, we were disappointed. Spencer was, too. I think that we both were hoping that the box would have been filled with money or something.

And I don't know why I decided to take the dolls home. Maybe I was just curious. Maybe I thought the dolls might be valuable.

But something happened as soon as I got the dolls home.

Something strange.

Soon . . . *very* soon . . . Spencer and I would both be wishing that we'd *never* found those dolls!

2

It started to rain on the way home.

"Great," Spencer groaned as he gazed up at the ash-gray sky. "There goes my day of fishing."

"Well, we didn't find very many worms in the first place," I said.

"Yeah. Too bad I can't fish with dolls."

It didn't rain very hard, but by the time we got home, Spencer and I were soaked. I'd held the dolls close to me, and bent forward to shield them with my body, so they didn't get very wet at all.

Mom was in the kitchen when we walked in the door. Rufus, our brown and white cocker spaniel, ran around our feet. Rufus is a great dog, and he's really friendly.

"Look what we found buried in the ground!" I exclaimed, holding up the dolls for Mom to see.

"Make sure you both take your shoes off," Mom said, ignoring the dolls. "They're full of mud."

I kicked off my shoes and pulled my wet hair back away from my face.

"But look at these *dolls*," I said, as I walked into the kitchen. "We found them buried in the ground in an old box."

Mom looked at the dolls. "Are you sure you weren't digging in some old garbage dump?" she asked.

"No," I replied, shaking my head. "We were out in the woods digging for worms. We found an old box in the ground. When we opened it up, these two dolls were inside."

"Well, someone probably threw them away," Mom said. She looked me up and down. "Good grief, Serena! You're soaked! Get out of those wet clothes before you catch a cold!"

I walked through the kitchen and into the living room, and placed the dolls on the couch. I turned and walked down the hall and into my bedroom, changed into dry pants and a shirt, then carried my wet clothing into the bathroom to hang them over the shower curtain rod to dry.

I went back to the living room to get the dolls, intending to take them into the garage and clean them up.

But when I went to the couch, one of the dolls was missing!

"Spencer!" I called down the hall. He's always playing tricks on me and trying to scare me. I thought that maybe he hid the doll just to make me mad.

Spencer's head appeared from his bedroom door. "What?"

"Did you do something with the boy doll?"

He shook his head. "No. I've been in my bedroom. Ask Mom." He disappeared back into his room.

I walked into the kitchen.

"Mom . . . have you seen my doll? The boy doll is missing."

"I've been in the kitchen," she said. "Didn't you just have it?"

"Yeah," I said. "But I put both of them on the couch. One of them is missing."

"I haven't seen it," Mom said.

This is too weird, I thought. *How can a doll just disappear? It couldn't have just got up and walked away!*

Well, I was about to find the doll, all right.

And I was also about to find out something else.

The dolls we had found weren't just ordinary dolls.

In fact, they were terrifying.

Terrifying . . . and *dangerous*.

Something caught my eye outside the livingroom window.

Something that moved.

And when I saw what it was, I gasped.

3

The doll was outside . . . *and it was being carried by our cocker spaniel, Rufus!* He must have picked it up off the couch and took it outside.

"Oh, no!" I cried, and ran for the back door. Rufus chews things up sometimes, and I didn't want him ruining the doll.

I threw open the back door.

"Rufus!" I shouted. *"Get in here! Right now!"*

Rufus looked at me sheepishly. He knew that he'd been caught, and he hung his head as he slowly walked toward me. When he reached the door, he dropped the doll on the porch.

"Good boy," I said smiling, as I petted him on the head. It's hard to stay mad at Rufus. He really *is* a good dog. Rufus wagged his tail and scampered out into the yard. I noticed that it had finally stopped raining, which was a good thing. The doll would have been soaked by now.

I picked it up. Thankfully, Rufus hadn't started chewing on it, and the doll wasn't damaged.

It was then that I really took a good look at the doll's face.

And the first word that came to my mind was . . . *creepy*.

I don't know why. The doll just looked weird. Like it was almost alive or something. It didn't look like any other doll I had ever seen before in my life.

I carried it back through the kitchen where Mom was busy making a cake for the church bake sale. In the living room, the girl doll was right where I had left her on the couch.

I put down the smaller doll and picked up the girl doll. Again, I was struck by how eerie the face looked. There was something about these dolls that wasn't right . . . but I didn't know what it was.

Then, something happened that was more than creepy.

It was more than terrifying.

While I was holding up the girl doll, examining her face . . . *she winked at me!*

4

I dropped the doll onto the couch and screamed. Instantly, Mom was at my side.

"What's wrong?!" she asked.

"The doll!" I replied in shock. "It . . . it winked at me!"

"Don't be silly," Mom said. She reached down and picked up the doll. I took a step back.

"There's the reason it winked at you," she said. "The eyes move by themselves."

I peered closer and looked. Sure enough, the doll's eyelids closed when she was leaned backward.

"But . . . but she didn't have those kind of eyelids before!" I stammered. "She didn't!"

"Of course she did," Mom said. She handed me the doll. "I tell you, Serena. You have quite an imagination."

Mom didn't believe me!

I stared at the doll. Now it creeped me out even more. I just knew that something wasn't right about these dolls.

Why would someone go through the trouble to put the dolls in a box and bury them in ground? I wondered. It just didn't make sense.

Unless, of course, someone was trying to get rid of the dolls for some reason. They wanted to put them some place where no one would find them.

Or perhaps in a place where the dolls couldn't get out.

Don't be goofy, I told myself. *Dolls are dolls. Besides . . . they might be worth a lot of money.*

We live in Camden, Delaware, which isn't far from Dover, the state capitol. There's a really cool collectible store that has all kinds of different things like coins, stamps, old bottles . . . stuff like that. I wanted to take the dolls there to show the store owner. Maybe they would know something more about them.

However, that wasn't going to happen. Not today, anyway. Mom asked me to help her in the kitchen, and I spent the rest of the day cooking and baking with her. Spencer went fishing, but he didn't catch anything.

All in all, the day was pretty normal.

The night, however, was going to be anything but normal.

And it was all because of—you guessed it—those two dolls.

You see, I was about to find out that I was right.

Those two dolls weren't ordinary dolls at all. And if you get spooked easily, you're probably not going to want to go any farther.

Stop reading. NOW. I mean it.

Because what was about to happen that night still freaks me out to this very day . . .

5

Dad came home from work with pizza, which was totally cool. Mom had called Dad at work and said she was tired from baking and cooking all day, and asked him to pick up something for supper. We all munched on pizza while watching a movie on television.

Finally, it was time for bed. I had just pulled the covers back when Mom called out to me.

"Serena . . . come get your dolls and put them away."

To tell you the truth, I had forgotten about the dolls. I'd put them on a bookshelf in the living room where Rufus couldn't get at them.

I went out and took them from the shelf. Then I walked back into my bedroom and put the dolls on my dresser and climbed into bed. A few minutes later,

Mom came in, kissed me on the forehead, turned my bedroom light off, and left. Sometimes Mom lets me read in bed before I go to sleep, but tonight I was too tired.

However, as soon as all of the lights in the house went out, I realized that I would never get to sleep with those creepy dolls in my room. The moonlight shone through the window, and reflected off their faces. They looked even spookier than before.

I felt as if they were staring at me. Watching me.

I closed my eyes and tried to forget about the dolls, but it was impossible. Have you ever felt like someone was watching you? That's exactly what I felt like. I felt like I was being spied on.

Finally, after a few more minutes of trying to get to sleep, I slipped out of bed and walked to the dresser. I picked up both dolls, opened up my closet door, and tossed them inside. I couldn't see inside the closet, and I didn't care. I just wanted those dolls out of my sight.

I closed the door and climbed back into bed.

And fell asleep.

But not for long.

I must have just fallen asleep when I was awakened by a sound.

A scraping noise.

I pulled the sheets up to my chin, trembling with fear. Because I knew where the sounds were coming from.

My closet.

Then—

A voice!

A child's voice began speaking! And as I listened, my horror ballooned into all-out terror.

"We're coming for you, Serena! We're coming for you . . ."

6

I trembled in terror, and pulled the covers up to my eyes. The voice came again.

"We're coming for you, Serena. You'll never get away . . . never, ever, ever. . . ."

Talk about freaked! I just about fainted right then and there!

But I knew that what I was hearing was impossible.

Dolls can't talk, I told myself. *Dolls aren't real. They're toys.*

I heard a shuffling sound coming from the closet, but I couldn't see anything. I reached over slowly, found the light beside my bed, and clicked it on. My room was suddenly flooded with light, and I squinted as I looked at the closet door.

I listened, but I didn't hear anything more.

Had I only imagined I'd heard something?

No. I'd heard something, that was for sure.

Then. . . .

I heard another sound. More shuffling, coming from the closet.

Dolls aren't real, I told myself. *Not real. Not real.*

And so, I pulled the covers back. Very slowly, I swung my legs off the bed. My bare feet touched the wood floor. I stood up quietly.

The noise in the closet stopped, and I began thinking about the dolls.

Why had they been buried? I wondered. *If someone wanted to get rid of them, why didn't they just throw them out? Why go through the trouble of putting them in a box and burying them way out in the woods?*

The floor creaked beneath my feet as I tiptoed toward the closet. The shuffling sound had stopped, and I could hear my own heart pounding in my chest. Finally, I stood before the closet door. I stopped and listened.

Nothing.

With a shaking hand I reached out to grasp the door handle . . . but I never got that far.

Because in the next instant, the door suddenly flew open . . . *all by itself!*

7

Talk about scared! I jumped back out of the way of
the closet door—

Just as my brother leaped out!

His arms were raised above his head like he was
pretending to be a monster. His eyes were wide and
his mouth was open, but he didn't make a sound.

I yanked a pillow from my bed and swung it
over my head at Spencer. I was furious at him for
scaring me so badly.

"You screwball!" I hissed *"You scared me!"*

"That's what I was trying to do!" Spencer giggled
back.

"Just you wait," I snarled. "I'll get you back for
this!"

"Yeah, right," Spencer snickered. He darted out the door just as I hurled my pillow at him. It hit the door with a loud thump.

"Hey you guys," I heard Dad call out from down the hall. "Quit goofing off. It's bed time."

"Serena keeps bugging me," I heard Spencer say.

"Leave your brother alone," Mom said.

My jaw dropped open. I wasn't the one doing the bugging! It was Spencer!

But it was pointless to try and argue. Not tonight, anyway.

But I was mad. I vowed right then and there that I would find a way to get back at him.

I closed the closet door, walked back to my bed and slipped beneath the covers. Then I reached over and turned off the light.

I'll get him back, I thought, and I fell asleep scheming of ways to do it.

I woke up the next morning curled up in a ball beneath the covers. I could hear Mom in the kitchen, and Rufus prancing around on the kitchen floor, hoping for breakfast scraps. I could smell eggs and bacon and freshly brewed coffee.

But I wasn't ready to get up just yet, so I stayed in bed, beneath the covers. I heard Rufus come into my room, his paws scratching on the floor. I reached my

32

hand out from beneath the covers and patted his head. Then he trotted off, returning to the kitchen.

Finally, I pulled the covers back and stared up at the ceiling. Sunlight streamed through the window. Outside, the trees were still and silent.

I had forgotten all about Spencer's prank from the night before.

And I'd forgotten all about the two dolls.

Until—

I rolled sideways and climbed out of bed.

I stood.

Then I stopped.

And stared.

Fear welled up inside me, boiling up like a geyser. My whole body went stiff.

On my dresser, staring back at me, were. . . .

8

. . . the two dolls!

I tried to move, but I couldn't. I couldn't even gasp. Horror had me in a vise grip, and wouldn't let go.

The dolls sat side-by-side, facing me. They stared back at me like—

Wait a minute, I thought. *Dolls don't stare. They can't stare.*

But these dolls sure looked like they were staring. In fact, they looked like they were glaring at me.

I didn't move. I just stood there, looking at the dolls.

I put those dolls in the closet last night, I thought. *I know I did.*

So, how did they get on my dresser?

Mom suddenly appeared in the doorway. I jumped.

"Good morning," she said. "Breakfast is ready."

"Mom . . . did you put the two dolls on my dresser?"

Mom glanced across the room at the two dolls. She shook her head. "No," she replied. "You did last night, before you went to bed. Remember?"

"Yeah, but I got up and put them in the closet because they were freaking me out."

"Well, they didn't get back to the dresser all by themselves, Serena," she said. Then she was gone, walking back into the kitchen. Her words seemed to hang in the air.

They didn't get back to the dresser all by themselves, Serena.

Then how? Who could—

All of a sudden I knew. I knew *exactly* how the dolls got onto my dresser.

Spencer. Spencer had come back into my room after I fell asleep, got the dolls out of my closet, and put them on my dresser.

I stormed out of my bedroom and down the hall. Spencer was already up. He was still in his pajamas, sitting at his desk and working on his model airplane.

"That's *two* I owe you for!" I said sharply.

He turned. "What are you talking about?" he asked.

"I'm talking about you and your pranks. First, you scared me by hiding in my closet. Then, you put those two dolls on my dresser!"

Spencer looked at me like I was some sort of space alien. He shook his head.

"I don't know what you're talking about," he said. "I got in your closet . . . but I didn't do anything with those dolls."

"Then how did they get on my dresser?" I demanded.

"Serena, I'm telling you. I didn't put them there."

"You didn't? Really?"

Again, Spencer shook his head. "No," he replied.

And I believed him. I mean, Spencer likes to play jokes, but he wouldn't lie to me.

Now I was more freaked out than before. I was sure I had placed the dolls in my closet.

I was *positive*.

I went back into my bedroom and stood in front of my dresser. The dolls just sat there.

Silly, I told myself. *I was tired last night. I probably put the dolls there myself. That's it. It has to be. After all, dolls aren't real. They don't come alive, Serena.*

Wrong.

There was a reason those dolls were placed in a box and buried in the ground.

A good reason.

We had dug them up by accident . . . and I had no way of knowing about the horrifying things that were about to happen.

9

After breakfast, Spencer and I decided to ride our bikes to the collectibles store. I put the two dolls in my backpack and we left.

Where we live is really cool. Delaware is a really cool state. Camden isn't a very big city, and Delaware, compared to other states, is kind of small itself. The entire state has only three counties!

But there are lots of things to do here. On the weekends, when Mom and Dad aren't working, we go to Delaware Bay and go to the beach. In the summer, of course. It's far too cold in the winter to go to the beach! Sometimes we get some big snowstorms in the winter.

We rode downtown and parked our bikes beneath a big red and white awning. On the awning was a sign with black letters that read:

COLLECTIBLES
BUY-SELL-TRADE

"I'll bet you those dolls aren't worth a nickle," Spencer said as we opened the door. I slipped my backpack off and carried it under my arm.

"Yeah, you're probably right," I replied. "But there's no harm in checking. I saw a guy on television who bought a painting at a garage sale for five dollars, and it turned out to be worth millions!"

"That would be cool," Spencer said. Then he pointed at the backpack under my arm. "But those two dolls aren't worth a nickle. You watch."

The air inside the store was stale and old. It was like walking into an attic. There was junk all over the place. I mean . . . I guess it probably wasn't junk, but a lot of it sure looked like junk. There was a broken bicycle on a table with rusted handlebars and a flat tire. The seat was torn and the paint had chipped. The price on the bicycle was two hundred dollars!

Next to the bike was another table, cluttered with old lamps, books, a beat up typewriter, and a sewing machine that was ancient. The price on the sewing machine was four hundred dollars.

"Maybe I'm wrong," Spencer whispered. *"If people would pay four hundred bucks for an old sewing machine, maybe they'll spend a couple hundred for some old dolls."*

We walked up to the counter. So far, we hadn't seen anyone. There were no other customers, and no sign of the shopkeeper.

I placed my backpack on the counter, unzipped it, and pulled out the dolls. They looked just as creepy as ever. But as I looked around and saw how much money they wanted for a bunch of junk, I thought that, just maybe, the dolls really might be worth something. Spencer might be right: if someone would buy an old, broken sewing machine for four hundred dollars, they'd probably pay a lot for a couple of dirty old dolls.

There was a small bell on the counter, and Spencer hit it with his palm. A sharp *ding!* rang out.

"One moment, please," a woman's voice called out from somewhere. She sounded pleasant, and I figured that she was probably in some back room somewhere.

There was a shuffling of feet and the woman appeared.

"Sorry for the wait," she said as she made her way around tables piled with old stuff. She walked behind the counter. "And what can I help you two—"

She stopped speaking when she looked down and saw the dolls on the counter. Her eyes opened wide, and I thought for a moment they would fall out and roll away. She gasped, and jumped back, and her hands flew to her cheeks.

Then she started screaming.

10

The woman shrieked repeatedly as she cowered and pointed at the dolls on the counter.

"What?!?!" I cried. *"What is it?!?!"* I was worried, now. The lady was really frightened.

"There!" she screamed. "Get it away! Kill it!"

"Huh?" Spencer said.

"A spider!" the woman squealed, still pointing. "I *hate* spiders! I hate them!"

Spencer leaned forward, and I followed his lead.

On the counter, near the girl doll, was a spider no larger than a dime. Spencer gave it a hard slap and brushed it away.

The woman shrank in relief. "Oh, thank you, thank you," she gasped. "I know it's silly . . . but I've always been afraid of spiders, no matter how big they are."

"He's gone now," I said.

"Yes," the woman breathed. "Thank you again, young man."

"No problem," Spencer replied.

The woman seemed to calm down, and she stepped up to the counter and looked down. "Well," she said, looking at the dolls. "What have we here?"

"We were hoping you could tell us," I said, and I explained how we found the dolls.

"We were wondering if they were worth any money," Spencer said.

The woman picked up the boy doll and looked at it. "Hmmmm." She shook her head. "I'm afraid I don't know much about old dolls," she said. "But there is a woman who lives just outside of town that could probably help you. She collects dolls, and she would probably know if they were worth anything. She's a bit . . . umm . . . weird, I guess. But she's a very nice person."

She gave us directions, I packed up the dolls, and we left.

"Man, she sure flipped when she saw that spider," Spencer snickered as he hopped on his bike.

"I thought she was screaming at the dolls," I said.

We rode through the city, following the directions the lady at the store had given to us. After making several turns, we came to a small subdivision. The houses were crowded together until we reached the end of Oak street.

I skidded my bike to a stop, and Spencer did the same.

At the very end of Oak street sat one of the most bizarre houses I have ever seen in my life.

"Holy cow," Spencer whispered.

All we could do was stare.

11

The house looked like a giant dollhouse. It looked almost plastic, with shiny walls and shutters. Even the roof looked like it was made out of plastic.

"That's really weird," Spencer said. "Who would want to live in a house like that?"

I shook my head. "It sure looks strange. I wonder if the woman is home."

"I'm not sure if I want to know," Spencer said. "The place looks creepy."

"Well, all we have to do is see if she's home. Then we'll show her the dolls and see what she thinks."

Spencer didn't say anything, and I turned to look at him.

"I don't want to go up there," he said, nodding toward the strange house. "That house is just too weird. I'll bet the woman who lives inside is even weirder."

"Maybe so," I said. "But she's the only one who will know if these dolls are worth anything. Unless, of course, you're afraid."

Spencer turned. "I'm not afraid," he snapped. "Not at all. Come on."

He pedaled off and I started out after him. The house loomed large, and the closer we got, the stranger it looked. When I was little, I had a dollhouse made out of metal and plastic—and that's exactly what this house looked like. It looked like a gigantic dollhouse.

We stopped at the end of the driveway and leaned our bikes against a tree. I slipped off my backpack and carried it by the strap.

"Well, the lady at the collectibles store said she was kind of weird," Spencer said. "I guess a weird person would probably like to live in a weird house."

All of the curtains were drawn. The morning was warm, but there were no windows open, and no car in the driveway.

"She might not be home," I said. "But let's go knock anyway."

We walked up the driveway and stepped onto the cement porch, stopping at the front door.

"Even the door looks plastic," I whispered.

We waited for a moment, listening for sounds inside the house. We heard nothing.

I pressed the doorbell. From inside the house, we could hear the faint *ding-donggggg* fade away.

No one came.

I pressed the doorbell again.

Ding-donggggg. . . .

And then—

Footsteps.

"Someone is coming!" Spencer hissed.

Suddenly, the door opened . . . and we started screaming.

12

Before us stood a giant doll! A real, live, doll, as big as an adult, standing in the doorway! She had thick, auburn hair. Her cheeks were white and her eyes were a piercing blue.

I spun around, and bolted off the porch. Spencer did the same, and almost knocking me over in his attempt to get away.

"May I help you?" the doll asked.

I stopped in the yard and turned and looked back at the house. The doll remained in the doorway.

"You . . . you're a . . . a doll!" I exclaimed breathlessly.

The doll laughed. "Oh, I'm sorry," she said. "This is just a costume. I'm sorry if I frightened you. What can I help you with?"

"A costume?!?!" Spencer gasped. "But . . . but it's not even *close* to Halloween!"

"It's for a parade in another town," the woman explained. "It's their annual antiques festival, and every year, those of us who collect dolls dress up and walk in the parade."

"Yep, she's a weirdo," Spencer whispered. I poked him in the ribs with my elbow.

"We just had a question about a couple dolls that we found," I said. "The woman at the collectibles store said you might be able to help us out."

"Certainly!" the woman/doll replied eagerly. "Come inside, and I'll help you if I can."

We stepped onto the porch. I felt a little foolish for screaming and running, but, then again, it's not every day that you run into a giant doll!

Spencer and I walked into her house. It was amazing! Everywhere we looked, we saw dolls. Dolls sat on chairs, on the couch, even on the television. There were shelves lined with dolls, and pictures of dolls on the walls. She must have had more than a thousand dolls in her house.

"You sure have a lot of dolls," Spencer said.

The woman stopped in the living room. Standing there, she looked just like a doll would look. It was kind of spooky.

"Yes," she replied. "I've been collecting dolls since I was a little girl. I have over three thousand of them."

Three thousand?!?! I thought. *That's unbelievable!*

I held up my backpack, and began to unzip it. "I'm Serena," I said. "This is my brother, Spencer."

"It's nice to meet you both. I'm Mrs. Kirwin."

"We found two old dolls yesterday," I continued. "My brother and I were wondering if they might be worth any money."

"It's quite possible," the woman said. "Some old dolls, if they are in good condition, are worth a great deal of money."

I finished unzipping my backpack and reached inside. I pulled out the smaller, boy doll, and then the girl doll.

"We found them—"

I was interrupted by a shriek from the woman. She leapt back, her eyes widening in horror.

"It can't be!" she gasped. "No! It just can't be!"

"We were—" I tried to explain how we found the dolls, but I was again interrupted by the woman.

"Children! Do you have any idea what you've done?!?!"

I looked at Spencer, and he looked at me. I shrugged. "Well, we were just digging for worms and we found these dolls in a wooden box. Someone buried them."

"Put them away!" the woman shrieked, shielding her face as if she was being attacked. *"Put them away! Please!"*

I did as she asked, returning the dolls to my backpack and zipping it closed. The woman's shoulders slumped. She sighed in relief and collapsed onto the couch. She was surrounded by dozens of dolls, and she fit right in, dressed like she was as a doll.

"Sit down," she said wearily, so I looked for a chair that didn't have any dolls. There weren't any, so I sat on the floor. Spencer sat down next to me.

The woman took a deep breath, and began to speak. By the time she was finished, Spencer's face had gone completely white, and I had goose bumps from head to toe.

What Mrs. Kirwin told us about the two dolls was chilling. . . .

13

Mrs. Kirwin told us that a long time ago, there was a little girl who didn't have any friends. The other kids teased her mercilessly, so she played alone most of the time.

One year, she was given two dolls as a birthday gift. They became her only friends, and every night she would wish that the dolls would come alive.

And one day, they did. The girl didn't know how, or why, but the dolls came alive . . . sort of. The little girl had no idea how the dolls actually came alive, but she was soon very sorry that they had. The dolls were mean and nasty, and caused a lot of trouble. With every passing hour, the dolls seemed to grow more powerful and dangerous, causing even more trouble. The dolls would chase her and even try to bite her.

Finally, she had to put the dolls in a box and bury them.

"That's too freaky," Spencer said, after Mrs. Kirwin finished speaking.

"And these are the dolls that the girl buried?" I asked.

Mrs. Kirwin nodded. "They have to be. I know of no one else who would have had any reason to bury dolls in the ground."

"But these dolls haven't done anything," I said. "We've had them since yesterday, and nothing has happened."

"They will, very soon, I'm afraid," Mrs. Kirwin said. "It's only a matter of time." Her voice trembled, and I could tell that she was really scared. "I would help you," she continued, "but I am too old to be of much help."

Spencer looked at me and rolled his eyes. At first, he had been afraid. I had been, too. But now that I thought about it, the more I thought that the old woman was a little wacko.

"But they're just . . . just *dolls*," Spencer said. "They're made out of plastic. They can't come alive."

"Well, all I can say is that the two dolls caused a lot of trouble for that girl," Mrs. Kirwin said. "They have very strange powers. I'm afraid that if you don't put them back in the ground, bad things will start to happen."

"But are they worth any money?" Spencer asked. "Maybe we could sell them! Especially if they come alive. I bet they'd be worth a fortune!"

"I don't think that's a good idea," Mrs. Kirwin replied. "I think it would be best if you returned the dolls to the place you found them, and rebury them. If you decide to be foolish and not rid yourself of these dolls, I have one piece of advice: the dolls will become very sluggish if they are placed under water."

"They're pretty sluggish right now," Spencer said. I shot him a nasty glance. Sometimes, I wish he would be more polite.

"Why is that?" I asked. "What does water have to do with it?"

Mrs. Kirwin shook her head. "I have no idea. But I do know that the little girl used water to help stop the dolls."

We said good bye to Mrs. Kirwin, and left.

"Remember what I told you about those dolls," she shouted to us as we hopped onto our bikes. I couldn't help but think that Mrs. Kirwin seemed really afraid of what might happen.

"Okay," I shouted back, and Spencer and I began pedaling home.

"I think she's out of her mind," Spencer said.

"Me too," I agreed.

But there was something that made me a little uneasy. Something that made me a little nervous about the two dolls in my backpack.

Last night. The more thought about it, the more I was *certain* I put both dolls in the closet.

I *knew* I had.

So how did they get out? How did they get on my dresser?

The answer would come soon enough.

As a matter of fact, that very night, we would find out—in a terrifying way—that Mrs. Kirwin was right.

Of course, riding our bikes home, we had no way of knowing it at the time.

But soon.

That very night, I would discover that Mrs. Kirwin was telling the truth.

The dolls were about to come alive.

14

When we got home, Spencer went fishing. I took my backpack into my bedroom, took the dolls out, and laid them on my bed. As creepy as they looked, it was easy to imagine them coming to life and crawling around the room.

But I was sure that what Mrs. Kirwin had told us couldn't be true. I mean . . . I know that a lot of strange things can happen, but dolls don't come alive.

I picked up the two dolls and took them into the living room to show Mom.

"We met a lady today that said these dolls came to life a long time ago," I told her.

Mom smiled. "Uh-huh," she said with a laugh. "And do you believe it?"

I looked at the dolls.

"No," I said. "But I was really hoping that the dolls were worth some money."

I left the dolls in the living room and took Rufus into the backyard to play. He is such a silly dog. He loves to fetch sticks, but he won't bring them back. He just carries it around in his mouth, and you have to chase him down to get the stick back so you can throw it again.

Spencer came back later that afternoon. He didn't catch any fish even though he'd used all of his worms. Dad came home soon after, and we had dinner—fried chicken, corn on the cob, mashed potatoes, and cherry pie for dessert. I watched a movie on television, but it was boring, so I went to bed early and read a book . . . until I heard a noise at the foot of my bed.

It was a scraping sound, very soft and light, and right away I knew what—or who—it was.

Spencer.

He was going to try and scare me. He had crawled on the floor where I couldn't see him through my open bedroom door and to the foot of my bed.

And then I saw a movement. At the bottom of my bed, I saw the head of the doll slowly rising. Then I saw its hand reaching up.

I reached behind my head very slowly, and grabbed my pillow. Then I flung it as hard as I could.

"Knock it off, you creep!" I yelled. "And get out of my room!"

The pillow hit the doll and it clunked to the floor.

Suddenly, Spencer appeared in the hall. "What are you yelling about?" he said gruffly.

The blood slowly drained from my face.

Oh my gosh! It wasn't Spencer, after all! The doll had moved . . . all by itself!

"For heaven's sake," Mom replied. "Well, put them somewhere else." She leaned forward and kissed my forehead. "Good night." She turned and walked out of the bedroom.

"Where are you going to put them?" Spencer asked.

"Downstairs," I said. "In Dad's cedar chest."

Dad has a huge wood box—a cedar chest—that he made before Spencer and I were born. It's down in the basement, because Mom says we don't have enough room for it upstairs.

I plucked the dolls from my bed, carried them into the hall, and strode to the basement door. Spencer followed.

"You really saw that doll moving?" he asked, as we walked down the stairs. He was having a hard time believing me.

"Honest," I replied. "If I was kidding, I wouldn't be putting these dolls in a box in the basement."

At the bottom of the stairs, I turned on the light. It was cooler down here, and my skin broke out in gooseflesh. The cement floor was cold beneath my feet. The cedar chest sat on the other side of the basement, next to the washer and dryer and Dad's toolbox.

Spencer lifted the lid. The strong, sweet odor of cedar filled my nostrils. The large box was empty, and I dropped the dolls inside. Then Spencer closed the lid. There was no lock on the box, but the lid was heavy.

"There," I said confidently. "That'll keep the little buggers from going anywhere."

I went to bed, knowing that the dolls wouldn't be able to escape from the cedar chest with the heavy box of tools on top of it.

Before the night was over, however, I would find out just how wrong I was.

16

I was awakened by a noise in the hall.

I turned my head and looked at my alarm clock. It was almost five o'clock in the morning.

My bedroom was dark, but the streetlight outside glowed brightly and cast shadows across the room.

I listened for a moment, but didn't hear anything more. I closed my eyes.

There it was again. A creak in the hallway. Not loud. In fact, I could barely hear it. But I had heard something, that was for sure.

I strained my eyes to see. My room was gloomy, but I could make out the shadow of my dresser and the dark outline of my closet door. My bedroom door was open, and the hall glowed faintly from the nightlight near the kitchen.

I rose up slowly and propped myself up on my elbows.

Silence.

My eyes slowly adjusted to the darkened room. I could see a little better, now.

But there was nothing to see.

And nothing to hear, either. I could hear the faint murmur of crickets outside my window, but that was it.

I remained motionless, breathing softly, listening.

There it was again. A creaking sound, louder this time.

Closer.

I held my breath.

A shadow moved in the hall.

I exhaled softly, and took another deep breath.

The shadow grew larger.

My heart was pounding, and I was trembling. But I was too afraid to move.

I heard another creak, and suddenly, a large form appeared in the doorway, blocking the glow from the nightlight in the kitchen.

I gasped in horror.

It was a doll! The girl doll that I had placed in the box was now as big as an adult, standing in the doorway!

I tried to scream, but no sound would come out. I wanted to run, but where? The giant doll was blocking the door.

And then I heard the voice.

"Serena," the doll whispered in a singsong tempo. *"I'm coming for you, Serena. Yesssss, you."*

The doll came closer. I was now shaking so badly that I thought I was going to fall off the bed. Again, I tried to scream, but no sound came out.

"It's too late, Serena. I'm coming for you, and soon, you'll be one of us. Soon, you'll be a doll like me. Like us. Yessss, you'll be one of us."

The doll kept inching closer as she spoke, and when she reached the foot of the bed, I was finally able to scream.

And did I *ever!* I screamed as loud as I could, but the doll kept coming toward me!

"No, it's too late, Serena! It's too late! You're going to be one of us, Serena! One of us!"

And suddenly the doll was reaching out, grabbing for my arms.

"No!" I shrieked. "No, no, no! *Nooooooo!!!"*

17

I wasn't going to give up without a fight.

I kicked and thrashed and twisted, trying to break free from the doll's grasp.

"Serena. . . ." the doll was saying.

"No!" I shouted again with another savage kick. "I don't want to be a doll! I don't want to be a doll!"

"Serena. . . ."

"No! Stop! Stop!"

"Serena!"

I opened my eyes.

Mom!

The bedroom light was on, and I squinted. Mom had been holding my arms. She gently released them and brushed the hair from my eyes. She had a look of concern on her face. Dad appeared in the doorway in his silly blue pajamas. Next to him, Spencer stood, dazed and sleepy. He rubbed his eyes with his fists.

"Is everything all right?" Dad asked.

"She was having a nightmare," Mom said. "Are you okay, Serena?"

My heart was still pounding and I was shaking, but I was relieved. It had only been a bad dream.

"Yeah," I replied with a nod. "It was awful. A giant doll was attacking me. She wanted to turn me into a doll."

"Well, it was only a nightmare. Do you want me to leave the hall light on?"

"No," I replied. "I'm fine. I'm sure glad that it was only a dream."

Spencer disappeared, and Dad turned and walked away. Mom went to the kitchen and returned with a glass of water. She gave it to me.

"Thanks," I said, and I placed the glass on the stand beside my bed. Mom got up and walked to the door. Then she turned and reached for the light switch.

"Dolls can't come alive, Serena," she said gently. "Try and go back to sleep."

The light went out. Mom went back to bed.

I laid in bed for a long time, eyes open, staring up at the ceiling. All I could think about were those two dolls in the cedar chest, and how I had seen the girl doll climbing up the bottom of my bed.

And I kept thinking about what Mrs. Kirwin had told us, about the dolls coming to life and trying to attack her.

I made up my mind right then and there that, first thing in the morning, I was going to take the dolls back to the place where we had found them. I was going to bury them in the box and get rid of them, like Mrs. Kirwin had said.

But another thought bothered me.

What if it's already too late? What if the dolls get out of the cedar chest in the basement before morning? What then?

I was so worried about the dolls in the basement that I couldn't get back to sleep. I was tired, but I was just too freaked out.

What if the dolls could get out of the cedar chest?

Nonsense, I told myself. *Even if they really did come alive, they couldn't get out of the cedar chest.*

Could they?

There was only one way to know for sure. I would have to go down into the basement and see for myself. I would go downstairs and open up the chest, and I would see the dolls. Then I could get some sleep.

Yes, I thought. *That's what I'll do.*

I pulled back the covers and swung my legs to the floor, thinking that I was doing the right thing. But sometimes, when you think you're doing the right thing, you're not really doing what you should be doing. Sometimes when you think you're doing the right thing, you're doing the *wrong* thing.

And this was one of those times, as I was about to find out.

18

The floor squeaked softly beneath my feet as I tiptoed across the room. The tiny nightlight near the kitchen was bright enough so I could see my way around.

Down the hall, however, was a different story. The hall was dark and gloomy, and I knew that at the basement door, there wouldn't be much light at all.

I continued slowly, past my brother's room, then past Mom and Dad's room. There the hall turned and led to our game room, as well as the back door. Near the back door was the basement door.

I padded past the game room and stopped at the basement door, listening. The night was quiet, and all I could hear was the gentle seesawing of crickets outside.

The basement door was closed. I grasped the knob and turned it slowly. There was a click, and I pulled.

Silently, the door swung open. It used to make a loud squeak, but Mom oiled the hinges and now it didn't make any sound at all.

Looking down the staircase was like looking down into a dark pit. It was so black and dark that I couldn't even see the first step. I debated turning on the light, but I didn't want Mom or Dad or Spencer to know that I was awake. So, I decided to just wait for a moment to see if my eyes would get used to the inky blackness.

And it was then that I felt a hand grab my ankle.

19

Why I didn't scream my head off right then and there, I'll never know. Instead, I drew in a huge breath and spun.

Spencer!

I should have known. He had snuck up behind me, reached down, and grabbed my ankle to scare me!

"Gosh, you're jumpy," he whispered with a snicker.

"That's two things I'm going to get you back for!" I hissed. *"And I will get you back, I promise!"*

"Are you checking on the dolls?" he asked, ignoring my threat.

"Yeah," I replied. *"I was just making sure that the cedar chest would hold them."*

"I was wondering the same thing," Spencer said.

My anger faded. "So . . . you believe me that I saw the doll move at the foot of my bed?"

Spencer paused, then spoke. "I don't know. All I know is that I don't think you'd make up something like that."

"I wouldn't. And I'm going to go down to the cedar chest. I bet the dolls will be there. Then I'll be able to sleep better."

"You want me to go with you?" Spencer asked.

I had to think about it. Spencer can really be a creep, and I was still a little mad at him for scaring me like he did.

However, it might be good to have someone else with me in the basement, just in case something happened.

Just in case.

"Yeah," I said. "Let's both go."

A tiny beam of light suddenly appeared.

"I brought my pen light," Spencer said.

I was glad he did. The light was small, but it was bright enough for us to see the stairs.

"We can use this to see without having to turn any lights on," he said. "If Mom and Dad know that we're walking around in the middle of the night, they aren't going to be very happy."

He shined the light down the stairs, and I took a step down. Spencer did the same, and we slowly made our way to the basement.

At the bottom of the steps, we paused for a moment. Spencer raised his pen light and the tiny beam swept the room. Shadows danced and swayed. Here, in the murky belly of the house, there were no sounds at all. It was kind of eerie.

The large cedar chest came into view. It looked exactly as we'd left it.

"Come on," Spencer said, and we slowly walked across the cool cement, stopping at the cedar chest. I reached down, grasped the lid, and lifted. Spencer shined his light inside.

The dolls were gone!

20

I felt a chill run through my body like nothing I'd ever felt before. It was like ice cubes melting all over my skin. Spencer was shocked, too.

"They're not here!" he whispered. He snapped the light around the room, poking it around the washer and dryer and other odds and ends that were in the basement.

No dolls.

"Let's get out of here," I whispered.

"Then what?" Spencer asked. *"What are we going to do now?"* His voice trembled, and I knew that he really believed me, now.

"I don't know," I said softly. *"But maybe Mom or Dad moved the dolls. Maybe they put them somewhere else."*

"Why would they do that?" Spencer asked.

"I don't know," I said. I really tried to believe that Mom or Dad did something with the dolls.

But I knew that it wasn't true.

"Let's go," I continued. "Let's go back to bed. In the morning, we'll search for the dolls."

We turned and walked back to the stairs. All the while, Spencer shined his light about, on the lookout for the two missing dolls.

We tiptoed up the stairs and I closed the basement door behind us. I turned and looked out the back door window. The eastern sky was turning pink. The sun would be up soon. For a moment, I was hopeful.

Hopeful that I wouldn't have to spend the rest of the night in darkness, wondering where those two dolls were.

Spencer went back into his room, and I went back to mine. I climbed into bed and pulled the covers up to my chin.

But there was no way I was going back to sleep! I kept wondering where those dolls were. I imagined them beneath my bed, or in my closet, just waiting for me to fall asleep.

Then—

I looked out the window. The sky was beginning to brighten. Soon, Mom and Dad would be awake. I would tell them about what had happened, and they would have to believe me. After all . . . the dolls had disappeared.

And we would find them, I was sure. We would find them, and everything would be fine.

But that's not what would happen.

Because we wouldn't find the dolls.

The dolls would find *us*.

And if I thought what had happened already was bad, what was about to happen was ten times *worse*.

21

As the sun peeked over the trees, our house came alive. First, I heard the typical morning sounds of Mom and Dad waking up. Dad got up first, as usual, and brushed his teeth. Then he gargled, sounding very much like a sick water buffalo.

Mom walked by my bedroom on her way to the kitchen. I heard water running in the sink, and the refrigerator door opening.

And then Spencer was standing in my bedroom door. He was still in his pajamas, and his hair was wrecked, all jumbled about like soggy banana peels. He looked tired.

"See the dolls?" he asked.

"No," I said, slipping out of bed. "But we've got to tell Mom and Dad. They'll know what to do."

We walked into the kitchen together. Mom was peeling a hard-boiled egg over the sink.

"Hi guys," she said. "Want an egg?"

"Mom, there's something we have to tell you," I said. "It's important."

Mom stopped peeling the egg and gave us a suspicious glare. "Did you two break something?" she asked.

"No," Spencer said. "Worse."

Mom leaned closer. "What can be worse than breaking something?" Then, a look of alarm came over her face. "Are you two all right?"

"We're fine, Mom," I said. "It's about the dolls."

Mom looked puzzled, then she smiled. "Oh," she said. "You mean the nightmare you had last night."

"No," I replied. "The dolls we found two days ago. They're missing."

"You lost them?" Mom asked, and she continued peeling the egg.

"No, we didn't lose them," Spencer said. "They ran away somewhere. But we think they're in the house, and we all might be in a lot of trouble."

"Is that so?" Mom said with a smirk. I could tell that she didn't believe us.

"No, Mom, really," I said. "We put the dolls in Dad's cedar chest in the basement last night. Now they're gone. Mrs. Kirwin, the doll collector, says that if we don't rebury the dolls in the woods, we all could be in a lot of danger."

"I see," Mom said with a wide grin. "Dangerous dolls. I'll let you know if I see any."

"Mom!" Spencer cried. "You have to—"

I grabbed Spencer's arm and led him into the living room where Mom couldn't hear us.

"There's nothing we can say or do to make her believe us," I said. *"Until she sees one of the dolls herself, she isn't going to believe a word we say about dolls coming to life."*

"So what do we do?" Spencer asked. *"Should we search the house?"*

I shook my head. *"No,"* I replied quietly. *"I think we should go back to see Mrs. Kirwin. Maybe she would know what to do."*

"But what if the dolls are still here in the house?" Spencer asked. *"What if they attack Mom after Dad leaves for work?"*

I glanced at Mom in the kitchen. She was done peeling the eggs and was now slicing grapefruit. Dad came into the kitchen and complained, saying that his cholesterol was fine, that he'd really like some bacon and sausage. I don't know what 'cholesterol' is, but

Dad has a lot of it and Mom's been trying to make him get rid of it.

"We have to take the chance," I continued. *"Maybe if Mrs. Kirwin knows what's going on, she might be able to help."*

It was the only idea I had. I didn't have a clue where the dolls were, and I wasn't sure I wanted to know.

But Mrs. Kirwin seemed to know a lot about the dolls. After all, she had known the girl who had owned them. She would know what to do.

We ate breakfast. Hard-boiled eggs, oranges, bananas, and cereal. All the while Dad grumbled about how his cholesterol was just fine, and he would really rather have a big omelette. Mom just smiled and shook her head, and she didn't say anything.

After breakfast we rode our bikes across town and to the house where Mrs. Kirwin lived. Spencer rang the doorbell.

Twice.

Three times.

Four times.

And then we heard a sound from inside the house. It was very faint, but there was no mistake: it was a cry for help.

I tried the knob and the door opened. Mrs. Kirwin was in trouble, and I could only imagine the worst.

But Spencer and I were about to discover there was no way we could have imagined what we were about to find. . . .

22

"Mrs. Kirwin?" I called out.

It was so quiet. Dozens of dolls, on couches, chairs, and shelves, stared blankly at us.

I pushed the door open farther.

"Mrs. Kirwin?" I repeated, louder this time.

"Maybe the dolls ate her," Spencer whispered.

"Don't be a ninny!" I shot back. "Dolls don't eat people."

"Yeah," Spencer said sarcastically. "And they don't come alive, either."

He had a point.

"Mrs. Kirwin!" I shouted, then fell silent, straining to hear a response. We listened for a few moments, and then heard a faint voice.

"Here . . . in . . . here. . . ."

"She's upstairs!" Spencer said.

"Come on!" I said. "She sounds like she needs help!"

I pushed the door and it banged against the wall as we sprang into the house. A long hallway extended out of the living room and we raced through it. Then we came to a kitchen. There were dolls everywhere! On the counter, on the refrigerator . . . everywhere!

"Up there!" I said, pointing to a flight of stairs on the other side of the kitchen.

We sprinted across the room and started up the stairs two at a time. At the top of the steps we stopped.

A long hall opened up. There were closed doors along each wall, and a single, closed door at the end of the hall. There were no sounds.

We stood at the top of the stairs, listening. My heart pounded like a hammer.

"Mrs. Kirwin?" I called out.

From behind one of the closed doors, we heard a noise.

But which one? Where was she?

"Come on," I said. "Let's check each one."

We walked to the closest door. Spencer turned the knob and the door opened.

Inside the room there was nothing but dolls. There was no furniture, no bed, nothing . . . except dolls. There were dolls on the floor, dolls on shelves, even a doll hanging from the ceiling by strings. They all glared at us like we were intruders.

"Man," Spencer whispered. *"She wasn't kidding about having thousands of dolls."*

I turned and opened the door on the other side of the hall. Again, I was greeted by dolls glaring back at me. We tried every door in the hall, and didn't find any sign of Mrs. Kirwin.

But we were getting closer and closer to the door at the end of the hall.

"That has to be where she is," I said, and I walked up to the door and knocked.

"Mrs. Kirwin?" I said. "Mrs. Kirwin? It's me . . . Serena. Are you okay?"

A soft moan came from behind the door.

"Let's go in," I said. "She sounds like she needs help."

I turned the knob. There was a soft click and the door opened slightly. Then I pushed.

The door swung open with tired, high-pitched squeals from the hinges.

And all Spencer and I could do was gasp at the sight that was before us.

23

Once again, we were greeted by the still, dead eyes of hundreds of dolls . . . and something else.

Against the wall was a bed . . . with someone on it.

No, not some*one*.

Some*thing*.

What was on the bed looked like it had once been Mrs. Kirwin . . . but now she looked like she was changing. Her skin looked yellow and plastic. Her shoes were on the floor, and her feet had grown larger and rounder . . . like doll's feet.

"Mrs. . . . Mrs. Kirwin?" I stammered.

She moaned softly.

Slowly, I walked to the bed. Spencer followed.

Her face was large and round, her cheeks puffy and yellowed. Her eyes were open, blue and empty, gazing up at the ceiling in a daze. Her eyelids were waxy, and the skin on her forehead looked like paste.

"What . . . what's happening to her?" Spencer stuttered.

"She looks like she's turning into a doll," I said.

And then Mrs. Kirwin's lips moved a tiny bit.

"She's trying to say something!" Spencer said.

We leaned closer to listen.

"The . . . dolls . . ." she breathed. Her voice was so faint that I could barely make out the words. "The . . . dolls . . . must . . . be . . . stopped. . . ."

"Huh?" Spencer said.

And suddenly, it made sense. As crazy as it was, I knew what was happening.

"The dolls that we dug up! I'll bet that they are causing her to turn into a doll!"

"That's impossible!" Spencer said.

"No, it's not. It makes sense. I'll bet that the two dolls are coming more and more alive by the minute . . . while Mrs. Kirwin is becoming more like a doll. It's like they're stealing her energy. It'll only be a matter of time until she turns into a doll completely!"

"Yesssss," Mrs. Kirwin breathed, and she nodded her head a tiny bit.

"We've got to find those dolls," Spencer said.

"And we've got to bury them before it's too late," I echoed.

"They've got to be in our house somewhere," Spencer said. "But that means—"

A tidal wave of horror swelled up and crashed down on both of us at the same time.

If the dolls were at our house, and they were coming alive, they would be dangerous. There's no telling what they would do.

And the only one home was. . . .

Mom!

24

There wasn't a minute to lose.

"Let's go!" Spencer said.

"Don't worry," I said to Mrs. Kirwin. "We'll stop the dolls!"

We spun and flew out the door and down the hall, and bounded down the stairs.

"Wait!" I said, as Spencer reached the front door. "Let's call Mom on the phone! Then we can warn her!"

I found the telephone in the kitchen and dialed our number. It didn't ring. Instead, there was a strange series of tones, and then a recorded voice said that the number was out of service.

Out of service?!?! I thought. *No, it's not. It's our phone. It can't be out of service.*

I tried the number again. I received the same strange tones and the same chilling message.

"What's wrong?" Spencer asked.

"Our phone!" I exclaimed. "It's not working!"

"It's the dolls!" Spencer said. "I'll bet they've cut our telephone lines!"

And now I was *really* worried. I was really worried that we might already be too late.

What would the dolls do? I thought. *What could they do?*

Spencer and I flew out the door and leapt onto our bikes. I can't ever remember a time in my life when I had ever pedaled harder or faster. But no matter how fast we went, it didn't seem to be fast enough. We sailed past houses and yards, through town and over bridges. Past trees and fields.

Almost there, I thought. *Almost there. Just a few more blocks.*

I was breathing so hard my lungs hurt. My heart had to be pounding faster than my legs were pedaling. Once, I was going so fast I almost fell going around a corner.

"We're almost there!" Spencer shouted.

Just a few more blocks. Maybe we wouldn't be too late, after all. Maybe we could stop the dolls before—

Before what? I thought. *What would they do?*

Two more blocks. We sailed along the sidewalk, the wind whipping at my face and tossing my hair back. Almost there.   Around the corner to our block. . . .

My heart leapt into my throat as we rounded the corner. In our driveway was a police car.

We were too late! Something awful had happened!

25

The police car was parked right in front of our house. Its lights weren't flashing, and there weren't any police officers in sight. My sense of dread grew by the second. I knew that something terrible had happened.

I stopped pedaling and let my bike coast up to the curb behind the police car. It fell to the grass as I leapt off. I had to get into the house, and fast.

But before I reached the porch, I heard a man shouting.

"You! Hold it right there, you two!"

We stopped and turned toward the voice.

Next door, a policeman had emerged from the house. He was hurrying toward us.

"What is it?!?!" I asked, walking quickly toward him. "What's happened?!?!"

"Well, that's what I want to know," the policeman said. "What do you know about it?"

"It's all our fault!" I exclaimed. "Me and Spencer! Has anyone been hurt?!?!"

The policeman looked at me sternly, then glanced at Spencer. "So, you two are to blame?"

"Yeah," Spencer said sheepishly. "But we didn't know!"

"Is our Mom okay?" I asked. "Have the dolls hurt her?"

The policeman squinted at me, and cocked his head. "Dolls?" he asked.

"Yes," I said. "The ones that came to life. Spencer and I dug them up and now they're alive. We have to bury them so Mrs. Kirwin doesn't turn into a doll!"

The policeman suddenly let out a deep, heavy laugh. "I don't know about any dolls," he said, "but that's funny. That's really funny. What I want to know is who is responsible for putting toilet paper on that tree over there."

The policeman turned and pointed. Across the street, in the Miller's yard, a large tree held long strips of toilet paper. They twisted and writhed in the afternoon breeze, like thin white snakes.

The policeman looked back at us. "So," he said, "what do you know about that?"

Spencer and I shook our heads.

"Nothing," Spencer said, raising his hand. "Scout's honor. We didn't do it."

"We didn't, honest," I said. "We've been on the other side of town at Mrs. Kirwin's."

"Well, I don't know Mrs. Kirwin," the policeman said. "What I do know is that some kids vandalized that tree across the street, and I'm going to find out who."

"What's 'vandalized' mean?" Spencer asked.

"It means 'to destroy something," I answered. I turned to the police officer. "But we didn't do it! Honest! We didn't!"

The policeman looked at us. "You know, I believe you. I think it was a group of older kids that did it. Have you seen any around here?"

Spencer and I shook our heads. We hadn't seen anyone. Not lately, anyway.

"Well, if you see anyone, will you call the police station? We'd sure like to get to the bottom of this."

I assured him that we would, and then he climbed into the patrol car and drove off.

"Whew," Spencer said. "I thought we were going to get into trouble for something we didn't even do!"

"Forget it!" I said. "We've got to find those dolls!"

We turned, and I was about to run to our house, when I saw something that stopped me in my tracks.

The girl doll was in the attic window, looking down at us!

26

"Spencer!" I gasped. I pointed at the doll in the attic window. "Look!"

The doll suddenly ducked out of sight.

"Did you see it?" I asked.

Spencer nodded, his eyes wide. "Yeah," he said.

We bolted across the porch and into the house.

"Mom!" I shouted. "Mom!"

There was no reply, and I grew fearful. Was Mom okay? Where was she?

"Mom! Mom! Where are you?!?!" Spencer and I shouted.

There was no answer. The house was silent. If Mom was in the house, she would have heard us. That is, of course, unless the dolls had done something terrible.

I walked into the kitchen. There was a note on the table.

"Spencer! Here!"

I read the note out loud. *"Spencer and Serena: I went grocery shopping. Please clean your rooms while I'm gone. Also, Rufus is in the backyard. Please check on him. I'll be home soon. Love, Mom."*

"Well," Spencer said, "at least we know that the dolls didn't eat her."

"The dolls wouldn't eat her," I said, rolling my eyes.

"Hey, you don't know," he replied.

He was right. I wasn't sure what the dolls could do.

I peered out the kitchen window and looked out. Rufus was in the yard, chasing a dragonfly. He didn't even know we'd come home.

"Let's go up to the attic," I said. "That's where the girl doll was in the window."

"What are we going to do if we find them?" Spencer asked.

Good question.

"I don't know," I said. I thought about it for a moment.

"We could try and throw water on them," Spencer said.

"But what if we miss?" I said. "We have no idea what the dolls are capable of."

We thought really hard.

"Wait a minute!" I exclaimed. "Let's put them in my backpack! If we can get them in my backpack, we can carry them down to the bathtub and put them in the water! After we get them wet, we can carry them back into the woods and bury them!"

I dashed into my bedroom and snapped up my backpack, then ran back into the kitchen.

"Ready?" I said.

Spencer nodded and looked up the stairs. "I guess so," he said.

We walked up the steps. When we reached the second floor, we stopped and stared at the attic door. It was closed.

"I wonder how they got in there," Spencer said.

"I have no idea," I replied.

Moving slowly, we walked to the door. I pressed my ear to the door and listened.

Nothing.

I looked at Spencer, and he looked at me. He nodded and said nothing.

I put my hand on the doorknob, then turned it. The door swung open . . . and what we saw in the middle of the attic was *haunting.* . . .

27

Our attic is filled with a bunch of old boxes and things that we don't use. Mom is always asking Dad to get rid of a bunch of stuff, but Dad says that we might need it someday.

One of those things is an old wooden rocking chair. We've had it ever since I can remember.

And today, it was sitting in the middle of the attic . . . with the dolls.

Both dolls were sitting in the chair, rocking very gently. They were still and silent, and there were no sounds except for the squeak of the chair as it moved back and forth. Spencer and I stood in the doorway, afraid to get any closer. At first, putting the dolls in the backpack seemed like a good idea.

Now, however, I wasn't so sure.

And there was something in the lap of the dolls, too. A piece of paper or something.

"What do we do now?" Spencer whispered.

"I don't know," I whispered back.

However, I *did* know. I knew that, somehow, we had to get the two dolls into the backpack, take them back into the woods, and bury them in the ground.

But how? Now that the two dolls were in the rocking chair, I wasn't sure I even wanted to get close to them.

Suddenly, the chair stopped rocking. It became very silent.

Then the paper fell from the chair and slid toward us.

"Serena!" Spencer gasped. *"Look!"* He pointed at the paper on the floor.

It was a picture! A picture of a little girl holding two dolls!

The same two dolls that were seated in the rocking chair!

"That must be the little girl that Mrs. Kirwin is talking about!" I said.

I reached down and picked up the photo. It was old and yellowed, and cracked with age. The girl in the picture was wearing a light-colored dress. Her hair was dark, and tight curls snaked to her shoulders. She held a doll in each arm.

"Too weird," Spencer said.

Then—

One of the dolls moved. Just a tiny bit, but we saw the slight flinch of the boy dolls' arm. Spencer and I jumped, and our fear grew. It was really freaky to think that the two dolls were somehow coming to life.

Terror welled up in my heart. It was weird: I felt both hot and cold at the same time. My teeth chattered.

"I'm not touching those things," Spencer said. I could hear the fear in his voice. He was just as scared as I was.

I looked at the backpack in my hands. If I was going to get the dolls in it, I would have to touch them—and that wasn't something that I really wanted to do.

"Okay," I said finally. "I have a plan. Come on."

I closed the attic door, and explained my idea to Spencer.

"You think it will really work?" Spencer asked.

I thought about it for a moment.

"It has to," I said quietly. "It just has to."

And the more I thought about it, the more I thought that it really was a good idea.

Unfortunately, the dolls had ideas of their own.

28

My plan went like this:

I would go downstairs to my bedroom and get the blanket from my bed. Spencer would go to his bedroom and get his baseball bat, just in case we had to protect ourselves. Then we would go back upstairs and into the attic, throw the blanket over the dolls, wrap them up, and take them downstairs into the bathroom. There, we could hold the bundle under the faucet in the bathtub. Hopefully, the water would soak through to the dolls and stop them from moving around . . . at least long enough for us to get them back to the forest. There, we would put them back into the box and rebury them.

We hurried downstairs. I pulled my yellow blanket off my bed, and bundled it up in my arms.

Spencer retrieved his wooden baseball bat from his closet. The two of us met up in the kitchen, and we discussed our plan.

"When we get upstairs, I'll open the attic door," I said. "You go in first with the bat."

"Why me?" Spencer asked.

"Because if something happens, you can use the bat to keep the dolls away. And if we can't get them into the blanket, we'll close the door and think of something else."

I'll admit it—I was scared. I knew Spencer was, too.

But we had to stop the dolls . . . and *fast*.

"Let's go," I said, and Spencer followed me to the stairs. We walked up the steps, Spencer with his baseball bat and me with my blanket.

At the top of the stairs we stopped.

There were noises coming from behind the attic door.

"They're moving around!" I whispered.

Spencer gripped his bat like he was ready to hit a home run. *"Let's get 'em!"* he said.

We started toward the attic door . . . then stopped.

The door was opening!

The attic door swung open farther . . . and we knew right then and there that a baseball bat and a blanket would be no match for what we saw.

29

As the attic door swung open, the dolls came into view. They were standing side by side, arms outstretched, like they were reaching for us.

Strangest of all, however, was the fact that the dolls weren't touching the ground! They hovered a few inches from the floor, like they were suspended from strings. While we watched, they swayed slowly back and forth, and I could see their fingers wriggling. It was clear that the dolls seemed to be coming more and more alive with every passing minute.

"N . . . now . . . now what do we do?" Spencer stammered quietly.

"We've got to keep them in the attic," I said. "We can't let them get out of there. Give me the bat."

Spencer handed it to me. *"What are you going to do?"* he said.

Without saying anything, I suddenly bolted toward the open attic door. I carried the bat with one hand like a sword, ready to defend myself.

The dolls attacked. Their legs moved, but slowly, methodically, like they were battery-powered. The dolls skittered inches above the ground as they came at me, but I grabbed the attic door and pulled it closed. It slammed shut with a loud bang, and I heard them hit. Then I could hear scrapes and scratches as the dolls tried to get out.

"That was close!" Spencer gasped from behind me.

"We've got to think fast!" I exclaimed. "We don't know what those dolls can do. They might even break the attic window and get outside that way."

"Let's just hope they don't break down the door," Spencer said.

No sooner had he said those words than there was a loud pounding from the closed attic door. I leapt away and joined Spencer at the top of the stairs.

There was another loud bang, and we could see the door shake.

"This isn't good," I said, my voice trembling.

Suddenly, there was a crash so loud that I thought the door would explode. Instead, it started to open inward, slowly, very slowly. . . .

The terror I felt was unlike anything I'd ever experienced. It was a feeling of silent panic that grew with every passing second. My whole body trembled as the door swung slowly open.

But the dolls were gone. The only things we could see were just the things that were in the attic, old odds and ends that have been there for years. In the middle of the room, the old rocking chair sat empty and motionless.

An eerie silence fell over the house. It was creepy.

We waited, breathless, knowing that something was about to happen. Just *what*, we didn't know. But we both could feel it.

And so we didn't move. We stood at the top of the stairs, waiting and watching, wondering. . . .

We didn't have to wait for long.

A noise came from the attic. It was a loud, slow, scraping sound. Spencer and I took a step back, our eyes glued to the attic.

Then—

A shadow. A large shadow loomed. The shuffling sound continued.

Suddenly, I gasped. I dropped the baseball bat. Spencer dropped the blanket.

The dolls had grown . . . *and now they were taller than adults!* They were so big that they almost touched the ceiling!

And when the girl doll came at us, she didn't move slow. She came at us with lightning speed, and suddenly, Spencer and I found ourselves in the tight grip of her plastic hands.

We'd been captured!

30

We struggled and screamed. The doll held my arm tightly, and with the other, she had pinned Spencer to the floor.

I twisted sideways and managed to free myself. Then I grabbed Spencer's foot.

"Come on!" I yelled. I tried pushing the doll away, but I had to be careful to stay away from her arm. The doll was swinging her hand back and forth, reaching for me.

"Help me, Serena!" Spencer shrieked.

"I'm trying!" I shouted back. *"I'm trying!"*

I heard a noise from behind me, and turned in time to see the boy doll coming toward us. I knew right away that if we didn't escape now, the dolls would have us for good. And I didn't even want to think about what would happen then.

I pulled Spencer's foot while he struggled to break away. The doll swung her arm and I ducked, and then I lunged forward and gave her a push with all my might.

The doll lost her balance, and I seized the opportunity.

"Now, Spencer!" I screeched. *"Get up! Get up!"*

Spencer twisted sideways and sat up, then leapt to his feet. The girl doll had regained her balance and tried to grab us, but I was already half way to the stairs. Spencer ducked and escaped her grasp. The *boy* doll suddenly attacked, his arms outstretched, reaching for Spencer, but Spencer was too quick. In one giant leap, he was on his way down the stairs.

I made it to the bottom of the stairs. Spencer was right behind me.

And at the top of the stairs—

The dolls.

Both of them were glaring down at us, their eyes burning with anger.

But they couldn't come down! They were too big and clumsy to manage the stairs.

"Now what?!?!" Spencer exclaimed.

"We've got to get somewhere where we'll be safe!" I replied.

"My bedroom!" he said.

I shook my head. "They'll be able to break down the door!" I said.

At the top of the stairs, we could hear the two dolls banging around.

Suddenly, Spencer pointed. "Oh no!" he shouted.

At the top of the stairs, the dolls had stopped moving. However—

They were shrinking! The dolls were getting smaller, shrinking as we watched!

"We've got to get out of here! Let's get out of the house! Then we can go for help!"

We sprang across the living room. I shot a glance over my shoulder, only to see the two dolls beginning to make their way down the stairs. They had shrunk, and now they were about as big as I was.

I snapped back around just as Spencer reached the front door. I was so relieved! We could run next door and call for help. We would be safe.

Spencer grasped the doorknob, then he paused for a moment. Then he grabbed the doorknob with both hands.

"What's wrong?!?!?" I squealed. "Open the door! Hurry!"

"It . . . it won't open!" Spencer shrieked. "I can turn the knob, but the door won't open!"

I placed my hands over his, and we both struggled to open the door. The knob turned, but the door wouldn't budge.

"It's the dolls!" Spencer cried. "They must be using their powers to keep the door closed!"

I turned, only in time to see the two dolls reach the bottom of the stairs.

The problem was, there was no other way out of the house. With the dolls coming toward us, they blocked our way to the back door.

Spencer kept struggling with the doorknob. I turned back and saw the dolls looming closer and closer.

We were trapped!

31

"Spencer!" I cried. *"We've got to get away!"*

Spencer let go of the doorknob. *"The basement!"* he shouted. *"Let's go to the basement!"*

It was the only option we had. We couldn't get past the dolls and try to get out the back door, but we *could* make it down the hall and to the basement.

I *hoped* we could, anyway.

Spencer and I bolted at the same time. The dolls were still coming toward us, but they seemed to be floating above the floor. Their legs were moving back and forth like they were taking steps, but their feet weren't touching the floor. It was freaky.

In seconds, we were at the basement door—just in time. It was closing all by itself, and I was sure that somehow the dolls were doing it.

"*Go!*" I screamed. "*The dolls are right behind us!*" Spencer went down the steps two at a time. I was right behind him. I grabbed the doorknob and slammed the basement door behind me. It didn't lock from this side, but I didn't have time to worry about it.

Spencer was already down the stairs and standing on the basement floor. I bounded down the steps and stopped next to him.

The house was silent . . . but not for long.

Suddenly, we heard a pounding at the door at the basement door.

Slowly, the door began to open.

The dolls appeared.

I gasped.

The dolls had returned to their actual size, but they were floating in the air! They hovered several feet off the ground, suspended without any visible support. Their arms were outstretched, and their hands were clenching and unclenching. Their eyes seemed to glow, burning with fury. It was a horrible sight.

Spencer bent down and grabbed something.

"I'm getting really tired of you guys!" he shouted, and he threw something.

A softball! The ball sailed through the air and hit the boy doll! The doll was knocked back violently, and it thudded to the floor. Then the softball bounced against the hall wall and bounced back down the steps.

"You got him!" I shouted. "You got him!"

Without speaking, Spencer reached out and grabbed the softball as it bounced from the bottom step. He threw it again, aiming for the girl doll that had already started to float down the steps toward us.

Spencer hit his target easily, and the doll fell to the stairs. The softball bounced to the side, hit the wall, then bounded down the steps.

But what would we do now? I knew that the dolls wouldn't be stopped so easily, and if we didn't do something quick, we'd be trapped in the basement.

Then, there was no telling what would happen.

And when I turned and looked around the basement, I saw something that gave me hope.

A blanket. It was an old one that we used for picnics, but it was close . . . and it would work.

"Spencer!" I shouted. *"The blanket!"*

I didn't have to explain. Spencer knew that if we could get the dolls wrapped up in the blanket, then our original plan might work. With the dolls wrapped up, we could soak the blanket in water in the bathtub, then carry the dolls back into the forest and bury them.

I grabbed the blanket and unfolded it. Spencer grabbed one of the corners and we dashed up the steps, quickly draping the blanket over the girl doll. Then Spencer darted to the top of the steps. He kicked the boy doll. It tumbled down to me, and I quickly wrapped it up in the blanket. Then I bundled up the whole mess.

"To the bathtub!" I shouted. "Get the water running!"

Spencer was already on his way. With the bundle of dolls in my arms, I sprang up the steps and down the hall. Then I turned and went into the bathroom. I could feel the dolls beneath the blanket, struggling to get free.

"Hurry!" I said. "It won't be long before they start to grow again!"

Spencer kneeled at the bathtub, grabbed the hot and cold water knobs, and twisted them both at the same time. Water gushed from the faucet, and I knelt down and held the bundle beneath the flowing stream.

Water soaked the blanket. I could still feel the dolls kicking and thrashing, harder now, and it was difficult to hold onto them.

"Something's wrong!" I said. "It's . . . it's not working!"

One of the dolls gave a swift kick, and part of the blanket came off. It was the girl doll, and she reached out with her plastic hand and grabbed my wrist. She clamped down so hard that I winced in pain. I tried to pull my hand away, but the doll only gripped tighter.

"Why isn't the water stopping them?!?!" Spencer shouted.

"I don't know!" I screamed. "Help! She's got me!"

And that's when I realized that we'd made a big mistake. We shouldn't have tried to bundle up the dolls. We should have tried to get out of the house and go for help.

Now, however, it was too late. As I held the dolls under the faucet, unable to pull away from the tight grasp of the girl doll, I knew that we were out of options.

The dolls were going to win.

32

"Spencer!" I shouted. *"Help me! It's got me!"*

Spencer jumped into the bathtub, grabbed the doll's arm, and tried to pull it away. My arm was turning red from being gripped so tightly.

The water continued to pour over the bundle. Suddenly, the dolls stopped kicking and thrashing. The girl doll released her grip on my arm, and I pulled it away.

"Hey!" I said, still holding the dolls under the water. "It's working! I think the water paralyzed the dolls!"

I placed the dolls in the tub, making sure that the water from the faucet continued to pour over them. Then I carefully re-wrapped the blanket around them.

"We've got to get them to the forest," I said.

"It's too bad we couldn't carry them in a bucket of water," Spencer said.

My eyes grew wide. "That's it!" I exclaimed. "Spencer! You're a genius!"

"What?" he said.

"Let's fill a bucket with water and put the dolls in it! Then we can carry them to the forest and rebury them! There's no way they would be able to come alive if they're under water!"

"Yeah!" Spencer cried. "I'll go get one!"

He ran out of the bathroom and disappeared. I sat down on the edge of the bathtub, watching the water run from the faucet and pour over the bundle. It was soaked and unmoving.

And boy . . . you can't imagine how relieved I was. We'd stopped the dolls, and now we'd be able to get them back where they belonged—in the ground.

Spencer returned after a moment with a large red pail.

"That'll be perfect," I said, getting to my feet. I took the pail from Spencer and placed it in the tub. Then I grabbed the sopped bundle, placed it in the bucket, and held it under the faucet until it was filled to the top.

"That's perfect," Spencer said.

"Let's go," I said. "The sooner we get these things in the ground, the better. I just hope that we're not too late to save Mrs. Kirwin."

I lifted the bucket up. It was heavy, and water splashed over the sides and onto the tile floor.

"We'll have to take turns," I said. "I won't be able to carry this all the way out to the forest."

"Be careful," Spencer said.

"I will. Let's go."

I carried the bucket through the house, and we went out the back door. Outside, the sky was a bright blue, and the leaves on the trees shone in the sun.

I stepped off the back porch and onto the grass. Rufus was laying in the grass next to a stick. When he saw us, he stood up and wagged his tail.

"Rufus, inside!" I said, and I held the door open as he waddled through. I shut the door.

"Let's go," Spencer said.

Water sloshed over the sides of the bucket, as Spencer and I started the long hike through the field and into the woods.

Everything was going to be all right. Soon, the dolls would be back in the wooden box. They would be in the ground again, covered with dirt, where they would remain forever. I was so relieved that I must have been a little careless . . . because I didn't see the small stump nestled in the grass. I tumbled forward and fell, spilling the bucket of water—and the bundled dolls—all over the ground.

33

I landed on the bucket, which had already spilled its contents all over the ground. The bucket broke my fall and I rolled sideways, landing on the wet ground, soaking and muddying my clothes in the process. I jumped up.

The dolls had fallen out of the pail, and they, too, were on the ground. There was mud in the girl dolls' hair, and her face was streaked with dirt. The boy doll was just as dirty. Both were sopping wet from being submerged in water.

"No!" I cried.

Spencer was already gathering up the dolls. He stuffed them head first into the empty pail.

"Come on!" he said. "We won't have much time."

I scrambled to my feet, and the two of us began to run.   Spencer carried the pail, swinging it back and forth as we sprinted across the field.

"Don't drop it!" I shouted.

We reached the forest.   Spencer and I were still running like crazy.   We found the trail and ducked beneath branches and limbs   I wondered how long it would be before the dolls began to move around.

And what would they do?   Would they grow bigger, like they had done in our house?   Would they float in the air?   Just how dangerous *were* these dolls?

Every few moments, I caught a glance of the dolls in the bucket.   So far, they didn't appear to be moving. If we could just get to the place where the hole was dug. . . .

We wound through the forest at a furious pace.   It was hard to breathe, running as fast as we were.   But I knew we couldn't slow down.   I knew that at any moment, the dolls might come out of their trance-like state.

"We're not far!" Spencer shouted.   "The place where we found the dolls is up ahead!"

Spencer was still swinging the pail as he ran.   I caught a glimpse of the girl dolls' face.

Then her arm swung up and over the side of the bucket.

"Spencer!" I shrieked. "They're coming alive again! They're coming alive!"

Spencer glanced down at the bucket as he ran. Then he quickly looked up. "The hole is up ahead!" he shouted. "So is the box! I can see it!"

Over his shoulder, I saw the box sitting beside the hole, just as we'd left it. The lid was open. All we had to do was get the dolls inside, close the lid, lower it into the hole, and cover it back up.

The dolls were thrashing about in the pail now, and they looked angry.

We raced up to the box. As Spencer stopped, he grasped the bottom of the pail and upended it. The dolls tumbled out of the bucket . . . and landed in the box.

Immediately, both dolls tried to get out. The girl doll tried to get to her feet, but Spencer pushed her down. I grasped the lid and swung it closed, but the boy doll managed to reach out with his arm and block it.

"In the hole!" Spencer shouted. *"Get the dolls in the hole before they get out!"*

I pushed the wooden box and it tumbled into the hole. It landed upside down, spilling the dolls. Both of them were struggling like crazy, and Spencer and I started to kick dirt on top of them.

"Faster!" I shrieked, and I fell to my knees and pushed dirt into the hole. I could still see the dolls struggling to break free, but the box was on top of them and the hole was quickly filling with dirt.

In a few seconds, the dolls had vanished. We kept pushing more and more dirt into the hole, and we didn't stop until the hole was completely filled.

Finally, we stopped. My heart was pounding, and I was gasping for breath. My hands and knees were filthy, covered with dirt.

Spencer knelt on one knee. Sweat streamed down his forehead and he wiped it away with the sleeve of his shirt. Neither of us spoke for a long time.

Then, after we'd caught our breath, I looked up at Spencer. "No one is going to believe any of this," I whispered.

Spencer shook his head. "Yeah," he agreed. "Everyone would think we'd gone bonkers."

Suddenly, I gasped.

"Mrs. Kirwin!" I cried. *"We've got to find out if she's okay!"*

We leapt to our feet and raced home. Our bikes were in the garage, and we wasted no time. If we pedaled really fast, we could make it to Mrs. Kirwin's house in a few minutes. We were worried that we were too late, that we'd spent too much time trying to get the dolls back into the ground.

Was she okay? Had we succeeded?

We were about to find out.

34

We rounded the corner onto the street that led to Mrs. Kirwin's home. It was now late afternoon, and the small subdivision was bustling with activity. A man was mowing his lawn, and there were a few kids playing in their yards. A dog barked at us as we rode by.

We sped along, our eyes fixed on the house at the end of the block. No one paid any attention to us as we sped past.

We reached her driveway and leapt from our bikes. They tumbled to the grass and Spencer and I ran up to the house. I twisted the doorknob and pushed the door.

"Mrs. Kirwin!" I shouted as we darted inside. "Mrs. Kirwin!"

Dozens of dolls glared back at us from shelves and chairs, even from the floor. It was really weird. I have to admit that I was a little nervous. You would be, too, if you'd been through what we had. I mean, it's not every day that dolls come to life and attack you. I couldn't imagine what would happen if all of the dolls in Mrs. Kirwin's house came alive and came after us.

"Mrs. Kirwin?" I called out again.

The house was strangely silent. There were no sounds at all, except for the light hum of the refrigerator in the kitchen. Outside, we could hear kids playing in their yards, and the sound of a lawn sprinkler *tik-tik-tikking* from the house next door. Other than that—

Nothing.

"Come on," I said. "She's here somewhere. Probably still in her room."

We scrambled up the stairs. At the top of the steps we stopped and listened.

"Mrs. Kirwin?" I called out softly, watching her door for any movement, listening for any sounds.

Still, nothing.

We approached the door. It was open a tiny crack, and I pushed it open farther. The hinges squeaked and squealed as the inside of the room was revealed.

And when we saw Mrs. Kirwin on the bed, our worst fears were realized.

We were too late.

35

"Oh no!" I whispered.

We stared at the motionless form of Mrs. Kirwin.

"Is . . . is she dead?" Spencer asked.

"I don't know," I replied.

Slowly, I walked to the bed. Mrs. Kirwin was on her back, her arms folded over her waist, her fingers laced together.

"Look," I said, pointing at her face. "Her skin doesn't look plastic anymore. She looks human again."

Suddenly, her eyes flew open so abruptly that Spencer and I jumped. Mrs. Kirwin turned her head, then smiled.

"You're . . . you're okay!" I exclaimed.

Mrs. Kirwin yawned. "I must have fallen asleep," she said, and she slowly swung her legs off the side of the bed.

"We buried the dolls," I said. "We buried them in the same place we found them."

Mrs. Kirwin nodded. "I know," she said. "If you hadn't. . . ."

She didn't finish her sentence. She didn't need to. We knew what would have happened if we hadn't stopped the dolls.

"Tell me," she said, "how did you do it?"

"Serena wrapped them up in a blanket," Spencer said. "Then we held them under the faucet in the bathtub."

"Yeah," I said with a nod. "Then we put them in a bucket of water and carried them out to the forest. I tripped and fell, but we were able to get them into the box and bury them in the hole."

Mrs. Kirwin nodded and smiled.

"Are you sure they won't be able to get out?" Spencer asked.

"Not unless they're dug up again," Mrs. Kirwin said.

"Well, don't worry about us," I said. "We won't be digging holes anywhere near that place again."

I glanced around Mrs. Kirwin's room. Like the rest of the house, there were dolls everywhere. On the walls were several old pictures. Mrs. Kirwin noticed me looking at them.

"Pictures of my family, long ago," she said. "When I was a little girl."

All of the pictures were black and white photos, and many of them had yellowed over time.

Suddenly, I gasped, pointing to a picture of a young girl. Spencer looked where I was pointing, and he, too, gasped. We spun and looked at Mrs. Kirwin.

She nodded. "Yes," she said. "It is true. That is a picture of me, long ago. Now you know the truth."

I looked back at the picture of the young girl. She was wearing a dress, and her hair was shoulder-length and curly. The girl in the picture, of course, was a picture of Mrs. Kirwin . . . *but it was also the same girl in the picture that the dolls had! The picture that the dolls in our attic had been looking at!*

"Let's go downstairs," Mrs. Kirwin said. "And I'll tell you everything."

36

Downstairs, Spencer and I sat on the floor in the living room. Mrs. Kirwin sat on a chair, and she began to explain.

"What I told you about the little girl was true," she said. "But I didn't tell you that the little girl was me. I was such a lonely, lonely little girl. I had no friends, except for my dolls. Every night, before I went to sleep, I would wish on a star. I wished that my dolls would come to life, so I would have *real* friends."

"And your wish came true?" I said.

Mrs. Kirwin nodded. "Yes," she said. "But I expected the dolls to be my friends. I didn't know they would turn against me. You see, the more the dolls came alive, the more I began to look like a doll. I realized very soon that the dolls were draining the life

151

from me. They were stealing it. They were greedy and mean, and I knew that if I didn't stop them, soon, I would be a doll. I wasn't sure exactly what the dolls would do, but I knew that it wouldn't be good."

"But how did you find out that water would stop them?" Spencer asked.

"I threw a bucket of water on them when they came after me," Mrs. Kirwin said. "At the time, I had no idea what the water would do. It stopped them instantly. However, within a few minutes, they began to come alive again. It was then that I knew I had to do something. The only thing I could think of was to bury them in a box and hope they wouldn't be able to make it out. And that's where they remained, until you two dug them up."

"We didn't mean to," I said. "It was an accident."

"I know," Mrs. Kirwin said. "But I'm glad that you reburied them." She smiled. "Sometimes, children, it is better if wishes don't come true. Nothing is truly free, and all dreams have a price. Remember that."

We left Mrs. Kirwin's house and talked while we pedaled home.

"Do you really think that she brought those dolls alive by wishing?" Spencer asked.

"Yeah," I said. "I guess I do. How else would you explain it?"

"I don't know," Spencer said. "But I'm never going to wish for anything to come alive. Ever. I think I'm just going to wish for a million dollars."

"Remember what Mrs. Kirwin said," I reminded him. "She said that nothing is truly free, and every dream has a price."

"Yeah, but if I had a million dollars, I could use the money to pay the price," Spencer said smartly.

"But what would it cost to get the million dollars?" I asked.

Spencer said nothing. He didn't have an answer.

We rounded the corner and turned onto our block. I was glad that the dolls were gone, and things could finally be back to normal.

But we'd forgotten one thing . . . and when we walked into our house, we realized that we were in big trouble.

37

The house was in shambles. While we'd been fighting off the dolls, all kinds of things had been tipped over. Nothing seemed to be broken, but I knew that if Mom came home and saw the mess, she'd be furious. We'd both be in time-outs until we graduated from high school!

We buzzed around the house like mad bees, putting pieces of furniture back into place, straightening the rug by the back door, and making sure that everything was back to normal. We finished just as Mom was pulling into the driveway.

"That was close," Spencer said as he rearranged a few magazines on the coffee table in the living room.

Outside, we heard the car door close. A few seconds later, Mom came through the door. She looked at us, and right away, she knew something was up.

"All right, you two," she said accusingly. "I know that look. What have you been up to?"

I looked at Spencer, and he looked at me.

"I can't tell a lie, Mom," I said. "You know those dolls we found in the ground?"

"Yes?"

"Well, they came alive and attacked us. But Mrs. Kirwin said that if we got them wet we could stop them long enough to rebury them in the ground."

"Yeah," Spencer chimed in. "Otherwise, Mrs. Kirwin would turn into a doll."

"The whole experience was awful," I said.

Mom looked at us like she was looking at two talking goldfish. Then she suddenly burst out with a fit of laughter.

"You two!" she said, still laughing. "I'm telling you . . . you guys should write your stories down in a book. You could call it 'Dangerous Dolls of Delaware' or something!"

She walked past us and went into the kitchen. I could still hear her chuckling under her breath. Spencer shrugged.

"I knew if we told her the truth, she wouldn't believe us," I whispered.

"Do you think those dolls will ever get out of the ground?" Spencer asked.

"I hope not," I said. "But I don't think they will. I think the chances of someone digging them up like we did aren't very good. After all, there aren't any houses in the forest, and not many people go there. But you never know," I said.

"Man, I hope I never see another doll again in my life," he said.

But there was something that Spencer forgot. Something that even I had forgot about until that very moment.

And that night, something was going to happen to Spencer that would nearly scare his skin off.

38

It was late at night. There was no moon, and the entire house was very, very dark. Spencer was sleeping soundly.

He was awakened by a sound coming from the foot of his bed. It was voice . . . a soft, childlike whisper.

"Spencer," the voice squeaked quietly. *"Spennnncerrrrrr. I'm here for youuuuuu, Spencerrrrr. I'm coming for you. There is no escape. . . ."*

A light clicked on, and Spencer started screaming his head off.

There was a doll at the bottom of his bed, creeping up the covers. It was shaking madly, moving up the bed sheets, coming closer and closer.

"Get away!" Spencer shrieked. "Mom! Dad! Help!"

And I started laughing . . . because it was me! I had dug one of my old dolls out of the closet and tiptoed into Spencer's room, and hid at the foot of his bed. I held the doll by the legs and pushed her head up, and the voice that Spencer heard was mine!

I jumped up, still holding the doll. "I got you!" I said. "I told you I would, when you didn't expect it! I got you back for scaring me with the dolls!"

Just then, Mom and Dad burst into the room.

"What's wrong?!?!" Dad exclaimed.

"Serena is teasing me!" Spencer said, pointing his finger at me.

"What are you doing out of bed at this hour, young lady?!?!" Mom demanded.

"I had to get back at Spencer for all of his pranks," I replied sheepishly.

"Go back to bed this minute," Dad ordered gruffly. "We'll talk about this in the morning."

And man, did I get into trouble. I tried to explain to Mom and Dad that I was just giving Spencer what he deserved, but they didn't care. They were really mad. I got grounded for a whole week! No television, no games . . . I couldn't even go to the library. I had to stay inside. No playing with friends, no nothing. The only thing I did was read. I really like books, but after a whole week of doing nothing but reading, I was pretty bored.

Until the mail came one day.

I was in my bedroom when Mom came in. She had a letter in her hand. "Something for you," she said, handing me the white envelope.

I was so excited! I hardly ever get any mail!

I took the letter and looked at the return address in the upper left hand corner.

"Mike Sherman!" I said out loud. I couldn't believe it. Mike Sherman is a friend I met last year. He lives in Vermont, but he came to Delaware last year for a family reunion. He told me all about Vermont, and how cool it was. Mike promised that if I ever came to Vermont in the winter, he would take me skiing.

And up until last week, we had been e-mailing each other almost every day. It was odd that I hadn't heard anything from him in so long.

Hurriedly, I opened the letter and began to read.

"Dear Serena," I whispered. *"I hope you're doing well. I had to write you this letter to tell you about something that happened to me and my friend. You're not going to believe it! I was going to e-mail you, but when you find out what's happened, you'll understand*

why I haven't. When you get a chance, call me on the phone, and I'll tell you about something that I discovered in my computer."

What did he discover in his computer? I wondered. *A virus?* I remember when my dad got a virus on his computer. He was really mad, and said he lost a lot of stuff.

When I was un-grounded on Saturday, the first thing I did was call Mike. His mom answered the phone.

"Hello Mrs. Sherman," I said. "It's Serena Boardman."

"Oh, hello, dear," she said. We talked for a few moments.

"Hold on, and I'll get Mike for you," she said. "I know he's excited to talk to you."

There was silence on the line, and then Mike's voice came across the wires.

"Serena!"

"Hi Mike!" I said.

"Wait until I tell you what just happened! You won't believe it!"

I thought about the two dolls and how they had come alive, and realized that I probably *would* believe him. After what Spencer and I had been through, I could believe just about anything.

"Tell me!" I said excitedly.

"Okay. You know what a vampire is, right?"

"Yeah," I said. "Like Dracula."

"Exactly," Mike said. "Well . . . what if I told you that they really exist?"

"Vampires?!?!" I replied. "But . . . they're just make-believe."

"In the real world, yes," he replied. "In the real world, vampires don't exist. But they do in computers!"

"What?!?!" I exclaimed. "Don't be silly!"

"I'm telling you the truth!" Mike insisted.

"You're not kidding me?" I replied.

"No way," he replied. "Are you sitting down?"

I walked over to my bed and sat. "Now I am," I said.

And Mike began at the beginning, the day he turned on his computer and discovered the Virtual Vampires of Vermont . . . .

next in the

AMERICAN CHILLERS

SERIES:

#13:

Virtual Vampires

of

Vermont

**turn the page to read a few
terrifying chapters!**

When most people think of vampires, they think of someone like Count Dracula. You know . . . someone dressed all in black with pasty-white skin, with two fangs protruding over cherry-red lips. A creature that sleeps during the day and prowls the night, searching for victims.

And most people—myself included—know that vampires are only real in books and movies. Vampires just don't exist.

But what if I told you that they really do exist? What if I told you that, yes, there really are vampires, that exist in another world . . . a world that is closer than you might think?

Would you believe me?

Because that's what this is about. Not just vampires . . . but *virtual* vampires. Vampires that are alive like you and me, living and breathing, walking and talking.

Now, I know what you're thinking. You're thinking that it's impossible. Hey . . . that's what I thought—at first.

But now I know the truth. And soon, you will, too.

My name is Mike Sherman, and I live in Stowe. It's a village in the state of Vermont. Lots of people vacation here, because there's all kinds of things to do . . . especially in the winter. Mt. Mansfield, which has the highest peak in Vermont, is a great place to ski and snowboard. In the winter, my friends and I go there a lot.

Something else I really like to do is tinker with computers. Oh, I like to use the computer for my homework and to play games, but I really like fixing computers and finding out how they work. When I grow up, I want to get a job repairing computers, or maybe even building them.

And that's how this whole thing got started: with a computer and a game.

I know it doesn't sound scary at all. But when you begin to understand just what happened and why, you'll realize why I was so frightened.

168

The computer that I have wasn't working right. It was an older one that my dad had given me. He had bought a new computer, and said that I could have his old one. It seemed to work okay for a while, but then it started acting up. It would shut down all by itself, and sometimes it would freeze up and I would lose all of my homework that I had been working on. There was something wrong with it, but I didn't know what it was.

Which wasn't that big of a deal. I could fix it, I was sure. I didn't think it would be much of a problem.

And if I hadn't received a birthday gift in the mail, things probably would have turned out a lot different than they did.

I got home from school one snowy November day to find a small package waiting for me. It was a birthday gift, sent by my aunt and uncle in California.

Even before I opened it, I was sure of what it was. They had asked me what I wanted for my birthday, and I told them I wanted a new car, or a computer game. Well, of course they weren't going to get me a new car! It's a great trick, and it works.

I opened up the package, and sure enough . . . it was a game for my computer. It was called 'Return of the Vampire'. On the front of the box was a picture of

169

an old brick castle. It looked really cool, and I couldn't wait to play it. *Return of the Vampire* looked like it would be an awesome game.

But it wasn't.

It wasn't awesome . . . because it wasn't a game.

It was real—and my rollercoaster ride of terror was about to begin.

2

I took the game into my bedroom and turned on my computer. The screen flashed to life, blinked a few times, and then started up. The computer game was on a CD-ROM, and I placed it in the tray and slid it shut. I could hear it whir as it spun round and round.

Suddenly, the computer screen went black, and it stayed that way.

Oh, come on, I thought. *Not again.*

I tried tapping the keys, but nothing happened. I clicked the mouse, but that didn't work either.

Just then, Jenny, my little sister, came into my room carrying a Barbie doll. She's seven, and four years younger than me. Sometimes she can be a real pest, but usually, she keeps to herself.

"Whatcha doin'?" she asked.

"Trying to get this thing working," I replied.

"Did you break it?"

I shook my head. "No. It's just getting old, and it doesn't work like it used to."

Jenny saw the computer game box on my desk. "Eeewww," she said. "That looks scary."

"I hope it is," I said, still tapping the keys. The computer screen remained dark. "If I can ever get this thing working right."

"My Barbie doll works right," she said, holding her doll up for me to see.

"Yeah, but I don't play with dolls," I said, growing increasingly frustrated with the broken computer.

"And it doesn't look like you're going to play on the computer, either," she said.

"Look," I said angrily. "Don't you have something else to do?"

Jenny shook her head. "Nope."

"Well, find something, or else I'm going to flush your Barbie doll down the toilet."

Jenny's eyes widened. The thought of her doll swirling down the toilet was horrifying. She spun and stormed off.

Well, that's one problem taken care of, I thought. *Now if I can only get this computer working.*

I turned the computer off, waited for a few minutes, then re-started it. While I was waiting, Mom came to my bedroom door. Jenny was standing next to her.

"Did you tell your sister that you were going to flush her Barbie down the toilet?" Mom asked.

"I was only kidding," I said. "She was bugging me."

"Well, you apologize right now." Mom folded her arms, and if there's one thing I've learned in my eleven years, it's this: when Mom folds her arms, she means business. There's no point arguing with her when she's standing in front of you with her arms crossed.

"I'm sorry, Jenny," I said, even though I was mad at her.

"Tell Barbie you're sorry," Jenny said, holding out her doll.

Good grief, I thought. But if apologized to her doll, maybe she would leave me alone. "I'm sorry, Barbie," I said, looking at the doll.

That seemed to satisfy both Mom and Jenny, and both of them walked away.

I worked on the computer for an hour, and I still couldn't get it to work. Soon, it was time to eat. The four of us—Mom, Dad, Jenny, and me—had dinner.

Jenny and I washed the dishes, and then I went back to work on the computer.

By bedtime, I still hadn't got it working right. I could get the machine to turn on, but it kept freezing up, and all I would get was a black screen. I was really bummed, because I wanted to play *Return of the Vampire*. I guessed I would have to wait until tomorrow to get the computer working.

Sometime in the night, I was awakened by a noise. It was a whirring sound, like a gentle hum. As I emerged from my sleep, I realized that it was.

My computer. I recognized the sound instantly.

But that's impossible!

It had turned on . . . all by itself!

I was confused. How did the computer turn itself on? I mean . . . I knew that it wasn't working right, and it was freezing up. Sometimes, it would even turn itself off.

But who ever heard of a computer turning itself on?

From where my bed was, I couldn't see the monitor, but the glow from the screen reflected against my bedroom wall. I pulled down the covers, slipped out of bed, and walked to my desk.

On the screen was the same brick castle that was on the box of the computer game. The words *Return of the Vampire* were at the top of the screen, and, at the bottom, the words *Play* and *Exit*.

How did this thing turn itself on? I wondered. I had worked on the computer for hours and didn't have any luck, and now, in the middle of the night, the computer had turned itself on and loaded the game . . . all by itself.

For a moment, I just stared at the screen. The brick castle sat alone, cold and dark. I wondered about the game and how it was played. I had read books about vampires, but I had never played any games. I was sure that this game was going to be really cool.

But it was late. If I played the game right now, I would be really tired when I got up in the morning. Not to mention the fact that if Mom or Dad found me playing a computer game in the middle of the night, they would probably take the computer away from me.

By moving the mouse, I placed the arrow-shaped cursor over the word *Exit*. I clicked it twice, and the castle vanished. Then I shut down the computer and went back to bed.

But something still bothered me.

How did the computer turn on all by itself? I didn't think it was possible. I've heard of computers that turn off all by themselves, but they're programmed to do it. I've never heard of a computer programmed to turn on by itself.

And in the morning—you guessed it—the computer was on. Only now, there were two words written on the screen. White letters in front of a black background read:

I'M WAITING.

It was kind of eerie. Who was waiting? For who?

I moved the mouse and the letters vanished. The image of the castle appeared.

Return of the Vampire. Play. Exit.

I left the computer on and went into the kitchen. Dad was at the table reading a newspaper and sipping coffee. Mom was drinking tea and watching a small television set on the top of the fridge. Jenny was eating a bowl of cereal.

"That computer you gave me sure is acting weird," I said to Dad.

He looked up from his paper. "That's why I gave it to you," he said.

"No," I replied. "I mean, it comes on all by itself. It happened last night. I shut it off, but it did it again."

"Hey, it's better than nothing," Dad said without looking up from the newspaper.

"Maybe it's stuck on," Mom said.

I shook my head. "No. If that was the case, it would be impossible to turn it off."

I went back into my bedroom and shut off the computer. Today was another school day, and I didn't have time to fool around with the computer. I'd have to wait until I got home to work on it.

And as I rode the bus, that is just what I figured I would do. After school was over, I would go home and find out just what was going on with the computer. I would fix it, and then I would finally be able to play the game.

Return of the Vampire.

Of course, if I knew then what I know now, I would have thrown that computer game—and the entire computer—into the lake.

And it all began when I got home and went into my bedroom. It was then that I realized something was really, really wrong.

Mom and Dad both work, and Jenny stays after school, which means that I get home first. Which is kind of cool, because that means that nobody is around to bug me if I'm busy working on something.

When I got home, I walked straight into my bedroom. Once again, my computer had turned itself on all by itself.

But that wasn't the weird part.

The weird part was what was on the screen. Big letters read:

MAY I COME IN?

That's all it said. The words remained in the center of the screen.

I sat down at my desk and moved the mouse. Instantly, the words disappeared. The castle came into view, along with the words *Play* and *Exit.*

Well, might as well play, I thought, hoping that the computer wouldn't crash.

I clicked *Play.* Nothing happened for a moment, and then the screen went dark.

Suddenly, white letters appeared on the black screen.

YOU DIDN'T ANSWER ME. MAY I COME IN?

What in the world? I thought. I placed my fingers on the keys and spoke as I typed. "No," I said.

What happened next was bizarre. The screen went black again, and there was a loud popping sound. Then there was an electrical buzz and a hum. The computer shut itself off.

Terrific, I thought. I had been hoping that the computer might somehow fix itself, but that wasn't going to happen.

I reached down and turned the computer on. I could hear it whir and begin to start up.

"Hey Mike!" a voice shouted from outside. "You home?!?!"

It was Hayley Winthrop. Hayley lives next door, and she's in the same grade I am.

I stood up and looked out the window. Hayley was standing in the yard, facing our house.

"Yeah," I said. "I'm trying to fix this dumb computer. Come on in."

I sat back down and heard the door open. Hayley came into my room.

"What's wrong with it?" she asked, standing next to my desk.

"I don't know," I replied, shaking my head. "It's acting weird. I got a new game called *Return of the Vampire,* and I really want to play it."

The computer was up and running again, but the screen was black.

Suddenly, words began to form.

WHO IS YOUR FRIEND?

I gasped.

"How . . . how did it know you're here?" I stammered. I scooted my chair back from the desk.

"What's that?" Hayley asked, pointing at the screen.

I shook my head. "I don't know. But it's acting like it knows that you're here."

"That's impossible," Hayley said. "It's just a computer."

NO, I'M NOT.

Hayley and I gasped.

"It . . . it heard me!" Hayley exclaimed.

Now I was getting scared. I've never heard of a computer that could actually respond like that.

I reached down and pressed the on/off button.

Nothing happened.

I pressed it again. Still nothing.

"Well, there's another way to shut it off," I said. I knelt down and reached behind the desk . . . but what I found sent waves of chills through my body.

"No!" I exclaimed. *"It's impossible! It's just not possible!"*

"What?" Hayley asked. "What's wrong, Mike?"

I held up the power cord, displaying the three prongs.

"It's not plugged in," I whispered. *"The computer is on . . . but it's not even plugged into the wall!"*

I double-checked, just to make sure that I hadn't grabbed the wrong cord.

Nope. The cord I had in my hand was connected to the back of the computer . . . and the computer was still on.

"Is . . . is there a battery in that thing?" Hayley asked.

I shook my head. "No," I answered. "There aren't any batteries in it."

"Then why is it still on?" Hayley said. Her voice quivered a tiny bit, and I could tell that she was more than a little nervous. I was, too.

"I don't know," I said.

The screen suddenly blinked to life. The castle appeared, along with the words *Play* and *Exit*.

"This is really strange," I said.

I sat down in my chair.

"What are you going to do?" Hayley asked.

"I'm going to play," I said. "I'm going to play the game and see what happens."

I moved the mouse and held the cursor over the word *Play*. Then I clicked.

The image of the castle faded slowly. Words appeared on the screen.

PLEASE ENTER YOUR NAME.

I entered my name by typing the keys.

PLEASE ENTER YOUR FRIEND'S NAME.

I typed in Hayley's name.

WELCOME, MIKE AND HAYLEY. ARE YOU READY TO PLAY?

I typed in the word *'yes'*.

PLEASE WAIT A MOMENT.

We waited. Nothing appeared to be happening.

184

Suddenly, a face on the screen began to appear. It was faint at first, but as we watched, it became clearer.

It was the face of a vampire . . . sort of.

It was a boy, maybe about my age. He had dark hair slicked back, and his face was very white. His eyes were two orbs of black coal. Two sharp fangs were barely visible, protruding over red lips.

And he spoke.

"Welcome, Mike and Hayley. Are you ready to play my game?"

I was about to type in the word 'yes', but the face on the screen spoke again.

"There is no need to type your response," the vampire said. *"All you need to do is speak."*

I raised my eyebrows. "Okay," I said. I couldn't help but have the strange feeling that the face on the screen could actually see us. Plus, I was still freaked out that the computer was running without electricity.

"Good," the face said. *"Now . . . place your hands to the screen."*

I raised my hand, and was about to place it on the screen. Hayley grabbed my arm and stopped me.

"Wait," she said. "I'm scared. I don't like this."

I looked down at the unplugged cord on the floor.

"Well?" the vampire said.

Hayley shook her head. *"I don't want to play,"* she whispered. *"I think we should shut the thing off."*

"It's too late," the vampire said with a laugh. *"Oh, it's much too late for that."*

Without warning, two hands lunged out from the computer screen! One hand grabbed my arm, and the other hand grabbed Hayley's arm. Then we were being pulled.

Hayley screamed, and I started yelling. "Let me go!" I shouted. "Let go!"

But it was useless. The hand were too strong, I know it sounds impossible, but we were being pulled into the computer!

It was then that I realized that we were no longer playing a game. *Return of the Vampire* wasn't a game . . . it was reality.

And our reality had just changed.

We were about to discover that we were no longer in the real world, but a different world altogether. A virtual world, where things existed that were beyond our imagination.

A horrifying world . . . of virtual vampires.

FUN FACTS ABOUT DELAWARE:

State Capitol: Dover

State Mineral: Sillimanite

State Nickname: The Diamond State

State Song: "Our Delaware"

State Bird: Blue Hen Chicken

State Motto: "Liberty and Independence"

State Tree: American Holly

State Insect: Ladybug

State Flower: Peach Blossom

Statehood: December 7th, 1787 (1st state)

FAMOUS DELAWAREANS!

Howard Pyle, author and artist

E.I. du Pont, Industrialist

Henry Heimlich, surgeon

Annie Cannon, astronomer

Valerie Bertinelli, actress

John Phillips, author

Robert M. Bird, author and playwright

Felix Darley, artist

Wilham Julius Johnson, basketball player

among many, many more!

AMERICAN CHILLERS
PICTURE PAGES!

Chiller fans!

AMERICAN CHILLERS
PICTURE PAGES!

Johnathan & Mrs. Rand, arriving in style for a book
signing at Barnes & Noble, Saginaw, Michigan!

AMERICAN CHILLERS
PICTURE PAGES!

With Debra Gantz at Hickory Woods Elementary!

AMERICAN CHILLERS
PICTURE PAGES!

Getting out the scare at Ann Arbor Public Library!

AMERICAN CHILLERS
PICTURE PAGES!

Chilling out at Pattengill Elementary!

AMERICAN CHILLERS
PICTURE PAGES!

A sellout performance at Roseville Public Library!

AMERICAN CHILLERS
PICTURE PAGES!

A warm welcome at Eastlawn Elementary!

AMERICAN CHILLERS
PICTURE PAGE!

A live teleconference with other schools over the internet!

AMERICAN CHILLERS PICTURE PAGE!

Question and answer session at Way Elementary!

AMERICAN CHILLERS

PICTURE PAGE!

With Mrs. Rand at Summer Scream at Clark's Ice
Cream and Yogurt, Berkley, Michigan, home of the
best ice cream in the WORLD!

AMERICAN CHILLERS
PICTURE PAGE!

Some friends at Pine Lake Elementary!

NEW!

WRITTEN AND READ ALOUD BY JOHNATHAN RAND!

available only on compact disc!

Beware! This special audio CD contains six bone-chilling stories written and read aloud by the master of spooky suspense! American Chillers author Johnathan Rand shares six original tales of terror, including *'The People of the Trees'*, *'The Mystery of Coyote Lake'*, *'Midnight Train'*, *'The Phone Call'*, *The House at the End of Gallows Lane'*, and the chilling poem *'Dark Night'*. Turn out the lights, find a comfortable place, and get ready to enter the strange and bizarre world of *CREEPY CAMPFIRE CHILLERS!*

only $9.99!
over 60 minutes of audio!

order online at *www.americanchillers.com*
or call toll-free: 1-888-420-4244!

About the author

Johnathan Rand is the author of the best-selling **'Chillers'** series, now with over 1,000,000 copies in print. In addition to the **'Chillers'** series, Rand is also the author of **'Ghost in the Graveyard',** a collection of thrilling, original short stories featuring *The Adventure Club.* (And don't forget to check out **www.ghostinthegraveyard.com** and read an **entire story** from 'Ghost in the Graveyard' *FREE!*) Plus, Mr. Rand has written and narrated a new series of thrilling audiobooks entitled 'CREEPY CAMPFIRE CHILLERS'. When Mr. Rand and his wife are not traveling to schools and book signings, they live in a small town in northern lower Michigan with their two dogs, Abby and Salty. He still writes all of his books in the wee hours of the morning, and still submits all manuscripts by mail. He is currently working on his newest series, entitled **'American Chillers'**. His popular website features hundreds of photographs, stories, and art work. Visit:

WWW.AMERICANCHILLERS.COM

Now available! Official
'American Chillers' Wearables,
including:

-Embroidered hats
-Embroidered T-Shirts
-Backpacks

Visit www.americanchillers.com to
order yours!

Join the official

AMERICAN CHILLERS

FAN CLUB!

Visit www.americanchillers.com for details

For information on personal appearances, motivational speaking engagements, or book signings, write to:

AudioCraft Publishing, Inc.
PO Box 281
Topinabee Island, MI 49791

or call
(231) 238-0297

About the cover art: This unique cover was designed and created by Michigan artists Darrin Brege and Mark Thompson.

Darrin Brege works as an animator by day, and is now applying his talents on the internet, creating various web sites and flash animations. He attended animation school in southern California in the early nineties, and over the years has created original characters and animations for Warner Bros (Space Jam), for Hasbro (Tonka Joe Multimedia line), Universal Pictures (Bullwinkle and Fractured Fairy Tales CD Roms), and Disney. Besides art, he and his wife Karen are improv performers featured weekly at Mark Ridley's Comedy Castle over the last eight years. Improvisational comedy has provided the groundwork for a successful voice over career as well. Darrin has dozens of characters and impersonations in his portfolio. Darrin and Karen have a son named Mick.

Mark Thompson has been a professional illustrator for 25 years. He has applied his talents with toy companies Hasbro and Mattel, along with creating art for automobile companies. His work has been seen from San Diego Seaworld to Kmart stores, as well as the Detroit Tigers and the renowned 'Screams' ice-cream parlor in Hell, Michigan. Mark currently is designing holiday crafts for a local company, as well as doing website design and digital art from his home studio. He loves sci-fi and monster art, and also collects comics for a hobby. He has two boys of his own, and they're BIG Chiller Fans!

All AudioCraft books are proudly printed, bound, and manufactured in the United States of America, utilizing American resources, labor, and materials.

USA